A FAMILY REUNION

THE 72 DEMONS
BOOK FIVE

JAMES E. WISHER

SAND HILL PUBLISHING

Edited by: Janie Linn Dullard

Cover art by: Stone Tower Studio

CHAPTER ONE

Daisuke hunched over the kitchen table in his Zurich apartment, eyes flicking between the yellowed pages of ancient tomes and the crinkled scrolls littering the table. His brow furrowed as he scanned the Infernal text, searching for anything of value amidst the esoteric nonsense.

Three days had passed since he finished off the cult of Abaddon and claimed the Devil Man's library. He didn't permanently claim it, he just claimed the right to study everything before handing it over to the Circle of Sorcery for safekeeping. That he hadn't mentioned his plan to the boss was a minor technical detail.

He took a deep breath and grimaced. The books even smelled evil. A mix of brimstone and sulfur had soaked into the pages over the years leaving their trademark stench behind. It reminded him of Ruq's fur when he was in rat form.

"Hey!" From his perch on the couch's arm, Ruq, currently in said rat form, voiced his objection to Daisuke's unflat-

1

tering thought. "I'm a demon. I can't help the way my fur smells. And you got mad when I tried the cologne Helena bought you last year."

"Yeah, brimstone, sulfur, and whatever the hell was in that stuff didn't make the nicest combination. And why are you watching TV instead of helping me?" Daisuke stood and stretched, his back popping after hours of reading. He walked around to look at the big-screen TV.

An infomercial for the latest and greatest wonder mop was rolling along full speed. The show's host, a florid fellow wearing the worst-looking toupee Daisuke had ever seen, went on about the absorbency of the new material.

"This is what you're watching? It's worse than the nonsense in the Devil Man's books. We should give the worthless things to some other demon cult. They might make the cultists *less* dangerous."

Ruq shook his little rat head without looking away. "I can't get over the crap humans peddle to each other. How is it the forces of Hell haven't taken over this world yet? We'd be doing you a favor."

Having seen the proclivities of numerous demon cults over the years, Daisuke couldn't agree. "I don't suppose you'd like to make yourself useful and help me search?"

"Not particularly, no. I want to see how many mops this clown sells. They have a live counter and the number is rising with depressing speed."

Daisuke rolled his eyes but didn't insist. They were technically on a break from work and just because he'd decided to use his rare time off to do research didn't mean Ruq shouldn't enjoy himself.

He returned to the table, reached for the next book, and sighed. Maybe this one would have something useful.

An hour later his hopes were dashed. It was nothing but mystic bullshit with no practical value from cover to cover. The Devil Man hadn't been an idiot, so why did he bother to collect all this nonsense? Was it the evil equivalent of people buying the latest bestseller to display on their bookshelf to impress their friends when they came for a visit?

"This is pointless," he muttered as he tossed the most recent book into the finished pile.

His eyes stung from the strain of reading and he rubbed them in the hopes of getting some moisture to counter the grittiness. Time for a change of pace. He'd been putting off talking to Remi's captured soul in the hope that stewing in the talisman's endless darkness would make the dead man eager to cooperate. Not that Remi had the power to refuse, but willing aid was generally faster than torturing an answer out of a spirit.

Daisuke fetched the dark wooden talisman from the storage area hidden in his bedroom wall. The crimson gem at the end of the black, rune-covered rod gleamed in the kitchen's light.

He took a deep breath to steady himself then said, "Remi."

The ghostly form of Remi's soul emerged partway from the crystal. His sunken, skull-like face and narrow shoulders trailed off into a smoky tail that remained tethered to the talisman.

"What do you want to know now? When will you free me from this vile prison?"

"Hey! Evil assholes don't get to complain about their fate in the afterlife. I'll free you when I'm confident I've squeezed every drop of useful information out of your worthless soul. Right now, I want you to tell me who else you sold demons to."

"There was a group of human traffickers out of Odessa and a smuggling ring out of Istanbul."

"What sort of demons did they buy?"

"The Odessa crew got a claw demon and the Istanbul gang wanted a death glider. Don't ask me why, I can't begin to guess what someone would want with the ugly things, but they paid well."

Daisuke returned Remi to the talisman, then jotted the information down on a notepad to be sure he didn't forget anything.

"Ruq, what's a death glider?"

"It's a demon that looks like a giant flying squirrel only with a skull head and sharp claws. Not much use in combat, though they could kill regular humans with no problem. They're mostly known for their exceptional eyesight. Hell-priests summon them to serve as lookouts."

"I bet smugglers could use them for the same purpose. I'll tell the boss and she can decide who to send after them."

Ruq switched the TV off and flew over to land on Daisuke's shoulder. "You know she's going to send you, right?"

Daisuke shook his head. "There are other agents strong enough to handle a couple weak demons. What say we take a walk?"

"I could use some cookies and ice cream," Ruq said.

"Good call. We'll go to the place near Arcane Books and Trinkets. After we eat, I can make my report. What time is it anyway?"

"Elevenish. Still early, but when did that ever stop us from eating junk?"

Daisuke would've sworn it was later than that. Time did not fly when you were reading boring, useless books.

He pulled on the thin leather gloves he wore to hide the burns on his arms before leaving his apartment. They set out for Sweet Treats, the best ice cream parlor in Zurich.

The bright sun and clear sky burned away the accumulated psychic gloom that came with reading demon books. A deep lungful of air not tinged with brimstone didn't hurt anything either. Daisuke walked down the bustling city streets. He weaved between throngs of tourists and smaller groups of locals. Ruq stayed invisible on his shoulder. Magic might be common knowledge, but Ruq was still a demon and he made people nervous. Best for everyone if he stayed out of sight in public.

It didn't take long to reach their destination. Soon the cheerful jingle of the bell above the door announced their arrival at Sweet Treats. The mouthwatering aroma of freshly baked waffle cones and other wonderfully unhealthy things filled the air. Ruq's tiny claws dug into Daisuke's shoulder.

"Steady," Daisuke muttered under his breath as he approached the glass display case, his eyes roving over the myriad flavors of ice cream. The cookie selection was underwhelming, but you couldn't go far wrong with chocolate chip.

A couple of British tourists were in line ahead of him. When they'd wandered off with their vanilla cones, the perky blonde behind the counter asked, "What can I get for you today?"

She was cute enough to tempt him into making a naughty reply, but he decided to behave himself. "Two large dark-chocolate waffle cones and a dozen chocolate-chip cookies."

The clerk favored him with a slightly disbelieving look then said, "Hope you're meeting someone. Otherwise you're going to have an awful stomachache."

He offered his best smile. "I'll be sharing, don't worry."

Daisuke paid, collected their treats, and exited the shop. He found an empty bench a short distance away from Arcane Books and Trinkets in an area largely free of people. He handed one of the waffle cones to Ruq. The imp appeared, snatched up the cone, and started slurping up the ice cream with a far-too-long tongue.

Table manners had never been Ruq's strong suit.

He was about to pop the last bite of cookie in his mouth when his cellphone rang. Daisuke wasn't expecting to hear from anyone today. He was supposed to be on a break, not that that meant anything if an emergency had cropped up.

When he saw the name on his screen he frowned. What in the world could Natsumi want? He hadn't heard a word from her since he left the family compound after defeating Vorgon.

CHAPTER TWO

Natsumi paced across the manicured grass of the Kugo estate's garden, her black leather boots crunching through the handful of leaves that had fallen from the maples. Her mind churned with worry for her missing father. He'd never just up and disappeared before. If he'd gone on a job for the family someone would've told her, even if the details needed to stay a secret. A job was unlikely since he still hadn't fully recovered from the battle with that insane Viking.

And that's what worried her. After losing his arm in battle, her father hadn't been the same. Though never a warm person, he'd gotten even colder. She feared depression had set in, especially once it became clear they had no way of regrowing his arm. Her imagination conjured all sorts of terrible possibilities, the worst of which being some kind of ritual suicide.

Natsumi clenched her fists, temper flaring. She had to do something!

Turning her stride toward the fire pit, she marched over,

tossed a couple nearby sticks of wood into the stone bowl, and clapped her hands together. "Oh spirits of fire, please accept this offering."

She snapped her fingers and the wood burst into flame.

When the fire was properly blazing, she asked, "Oh spirits, where can I find my father?"

The flames roared higher, sounding like a jet engine. But no voice spoke to her. The spirits had ignored her question. Again. They wouldn't do that unless her father had asked them to. The spirits of fire loved him more than any other in this world.

Natsumi grimaced and turned back toward the house. If the spirits refused to answer her question, she'd find another way. Maybe Uncle Yoshikazu would let her hire a wizard to cast a tracking spell. The Kugo clan had no use for such magic, but that didn't mean there weren't wizards in Japan who could cast them.

She strode down the stone path, mind racing as she tried to come up with an argument that might convince him. As far as Natsumi was concerned, his brother being missing should be enough all by itself. Whether it would work out as she wished was another matter altogether.

What would she do if he refused? Natsumi shook her head. Think positive!

At the top of the steps, she slid the rice paper door open and stepped inside. The clean, unadorned walls seemed more depressing than Zen as she climbed the stairs to the second floor where Uncle's office waited. It seemed like only yesterday she'd been climbing these stairs excited to receive her first official mission for the clan.

Natsumi encountered no servants as she approached the office. She paused in front of the door, taking a deep breath to compose herself. Going in halfcocked and ranting would do nothing to move her uncle. When she had her emotions as tamped down as they were going to get, she rapped on the door frame. The sound echoed through the hallway, sending a chill up her spine.

Not a great omen.

"Come in," Uncle Yoshikazu said.

Sliding the door open, Natsumi stepped inside and bowed. "Uncle Yoshikazu, do you have a moment?"

He sat behind his expansive desk, a single sheet of paper and a pen the only items on its surface. His expression was as hard and blank as a slab of marble. He wore loose robes out of consideration for the many injuries he'd suffered during the battle with Haakon. Even with magical healing, full recovery would take months.

He motioned for her to sit in the empty chair before him. "Speak your mind, Natsumi."

She settled in and said, "The fire spirits still refuse to tell me where my father is. I'd like to hire a wizard to cast a tracking spell. I fear he might be doing something drastic."

Uncle Yoshikazu leaned back and rubbed his eyes. "If the fire spirits refuse to reveal Rio's whereabouts, it means he is acting in accordance with their will. The spirits would never let anything happen to him. As for bringing in an outsider, don't even think of it. The Kugo clan would never live down such a display of weakness. Have faith in your father and the spirits. He'll return to us when the time is right."

Natsumi clenched her fists. She wanted to demand they act, that her father had to be depressed about his missing arm, but she knew such an outburst would do nothing to change her uncle's mind and would only make her look like a child.

She took a calming breath and spoke with forced composure. "Very well, Uncle. Thank you for speaking with me."

Yoshikazu smiled. "My brother is the strongest of us all. He would never abandon his duty to the clan. I don't know where he's gone, but I have full confidence whatever he's doing is for the best."

She knew her uncle's kind words were well meant, but they did nothing to settle her fear. Natsumi stood and bowed. "As you say, Uncle. I will endeavor to have faith. Excuse me."

Natsumi turned and exited the office, sliding the door shut behind her. It took no effort to say she'd have faith. Following through, on the other hand...

As Natsumi rushed through the hallway, her mind consumed by the need to know her father's fate, she nearly collided with Aunt Kiyoko.

She stopped just short of bowling the older woman over. "I'm so sorry, Aunt Kiyoko. Are you okay?"

"I'm fine, dear, but what's got you so worked up?"

Natsumi told her everything that happened. Sharing the story helped calm her racing thoughts. When she finished, she asked, "Do you think you could change Uncle Yoshikazu's mind?"

Aunt Kiyoko let out a soft chuckle. "You know your uncle better than that. Once he's made up his mind, nothing I might say will change it, especially when it's regarding the spirits or the clan's honor."

"Then what am I going to do?" Natsumi hated the desperation in her voice but couldn't help it.

Aunt Kiyoko thought for a moment then asked, "Have you considered reaching out to Daisuke? He could cast the spell easily and he certainly wouldn't care what Yoshikazu thought. He's only sort of an outsider, so the clan's honor should survive his help."

Natsumi's brows furrowed. She'd thought about her supposed cousin off and on since he left but still hadn't decided what to make of him. He was powerful and had no loyalty to the clan which meant he'd be perfect. "You think he'd do it?"

A little smile played about Aunt Kiyoko's lips. "He might do it just to spite Yoshikazu. Call him. If he refuses, you're no worse off."

A flicker of hope ignited within Natsumi's chest. "I will. Thank you, Aunt Kiyoko."

She gave her aunt a quick hug before hurrying outside. This wasn't the sort of call she wanted to make in the house.

Natsumi found the garden as empty as she'd left it. It was the perfect secluded spot to make her call. The soft breeze and chirping of birds did their best to soothe her nerves, but as she reached into her pocket to retrieve her phone, the anxiety came roaring back.

If Daisuke turned her down, she didn't know what she'd do.

With trembling fingers, Natsumi scrolled through her contacts until she found Daisuke's name. Taking a deep final breath, she tapped it.

CHAPTER THREE

D aisuke swallowed the last bite of his cookie and brushed the crumbs from his fingers before tapping the connect button on his phone. "Natsumi? What is it?"

"It's my father, he's gone missing. I need you to help me find him."

Of all the things she might've said, few would've surprised him more than that. No one was more dedicated to the Kugo clan than Rio. He was also the most powerful wielder of fire spirit magic in the world. Few people could take him anywhere he didn't want to go.

"Maybe you'd better tell me everything."

"There isn't much to tell. Two weeks ago he just left. He said good night the same as always and when I woke up, he was gone without a trace. I figured he went out on a job for Uncle Yoshikazu. He's not back to one hundred percent, but he can still do odds and ends to help out as he recovers. When he didn't come back, I asked the spirits where he was and they wouldn't tell me. I tried again today and they still refused."

"Why would they do that?" Daisuke knew enough about spirit magic to understand they wouldn't refuse a Kugo much, if anything.

"I can only think of one reason: Dad asked them not to. I spoke to Uncle Yoshikazu and he says we need to trust the spirits and wait for him to come back. I'm afraid he's going to do something drastic and end up not coming back at all. He hasn't been the same since he lost his arm."

Daisuke didn't care if Rio cut his head off to match his arm, but the pain in Natsumi's voice got to him. She wasn't as bad as the rest of the clan, temper aside.

"I can't just waltz back into Japan," Daisuke said. "The intrusion detection magic would pick me up in an instant and I'd have government agents on my tail the whole time."

"So you'll help me?"

Daisuke sighed and rubbed the bridge of his nose. "Did you not hear what I said about the risks? It's not that simple, Natsumi. I'll need to catch a flight and enter the proper way. It's already been two weeks, a couple more days won't make any difference."

"If you come in the official way, Uncle Yoshikazu will find out I disobeyed him."

Daisuke laughed. "You think he won't find out if I arrive using an illegal magical method? The Kugo clan will probably be assigned the job of hunting me down."

"What if I told you we have an undetectable way in? There's a gap in the ward only the four master clans know about." He said nothing and Natsumi continued. "He'll find out eventually and I'm sure I'll catch hell for it. But if you come in this way, we'll have time to find Dad."

Having a magical way in and out of Japan, should another

demon prison show up, was priceless. And Rio's disappear-
ance bothered him. Given what Daisuke knew about the
man, something more had to be going on. Curiosity had
always been a weakness of his. Besides, he kind of felt like he
owed Natsumi for her help during his last visit.

"Alright, I'm in. I need to talk to the boss first, but there
shouldn't be any issues."

"Thank you, Daisuke. I'll send you an image of a kanji
after we hang up. When you're close to Japan, picture it, and
you'll sense the gap in the magic."

"Okay, I'll meet you tomorrow at ten local time."

"I really appreciate you doing this. See you tomorrow."

He ended the call and a moment later a text with an
image attached arrived. It was a simple kanji with three
vertical lines, two horizontal lines, and a diagonal slash.

"You realize we're going to have to leave at three in the
morning," Ruq said.

Daisuke grimaced and stood. "Can't be helped. With any
luck we can find Rio and be home before the end of the day."

Ruq snorted a laugh. "Not a chance in hell."

Much as he hated to agree, Ruq was probably right.
Daisuke left the bench behind and set out for the Circle's
secret base. The walk only took ten minutes and soon
enough he unlocked the back door and stepped into the
familiar hall. It felt weird coming by when he hadn't been
summoned.

But shit happens. He stopped outside the door to the
boss's office, catching a faint whiff of tobacco smoke from
inside. Before he could knock she said, "Come in, Daisuke."

He opened the door and entered. His stunning employer,
the fallen angel Angelique, sat behind her desk, a lit cigarette

between her fingers. She wore her usual gray suit and her eyes glowed faintly golden.

"This is a surprise," the boss said. "Take a seat and tell me what brings you by on a rare day off."

He dropped into one of the two empty chairs. "Two things. First, Remi's soul told me where to find the last two demons the cult sold. Figured you'd want to send a team to deal with them. Second, I need some personal time. Natsumi called. Turns out something weird is going on with her dad. I agreed to help her track him down."

"I'm going to need some more details."

Daisuke obliged, making sure to leave nothing out of his report. "Anyway, it's cool, right?"

"A secret, secure way into Japan..." She nodded slowly. "That could be very useful. Do what you have to, but keep in touch. If an emergency comes up, I might need to call you in."

"I will," Daisuke said. "Thanks, Boss. Got a piece of paper? I'll copy the guidance rune for you."

She pulled a sheet of printer paper out of a desk drawer and handed him a pencil. Daisuke quickly drew the kanji and slid it back across the desk. "Here you go. I shouldn't be more than a couple days, barring major issues."

"Take your time and do it right. Nothing good happens when you rush on a job."

Daisuke knew that all too well.

CHAPTER FOUR

Daisuke tossed a final black t-shirt and pair of jeans into his trunk and snapped the lid closed. He wasn't bringing much on this trip, though he did have the Staff of Law and his supply of emergency rations. If something went wrong, he'd be ready.

A jaw-cracking yawn stretched Daisuke's face. He glanced at the clock beside his bed. Almost three in the morning. What a ludicrous hour to be awake. Much as he wanted to find Rio in a single day, maybe getting started a little later wouldn't have been the worst idea.

"I told you so." Ruq sat on the edge of the bed in rat form somehow looking smug despite the lack of expression.

Ignoring the jibe, Daisuke reverted the trunk to a metal card and slipped it into his wallet. With that he was ready to go. Well, almost ready. He grabbed his phone, typed out a short text addressed to both Jinx and Helena, and scheduled it to go out at seven local time.

"They're going to be pissed you didn't tell them in person," Ruq said.

"Helena's already pissed. She hasn't spoken to me since we left the boss's office after the fight with Abaddon's demon. And Jinx has been busy helping with Vixen's recovery. Anyway, this is easier since I don't want to bring them along on a family matter."

"Your funeral." Ruq flew up to his shoulder.

Daisuke stepped into a shadow and set off down the path to Japan. Miles flashed by in the space of a heartbeat until a flicker of power brought him up short. The wards surrounding Japan shimmered a few strides away. They were dim when viewed from the shadow paths but he still had no trouble seeing them.

Now to see if Natsumi knew what she was talking about.

Daisuke closed his eyes, visualizing the kanji. When the image had formed in complete detail, a spark appeared. That had to be the gap. It was so tiny he doubted it would be detectable even if you thought to look.

He slipped through the opening, careful not to touch the edge of the ward. He only had inches to spare on either side. Once he was through, Daisuke emerged from the shadow of a maple tree into a forest clearing. Birds chirped in the branches and a cool breeze carried the scent of grass.

Even better, no one was waiting to arrest him. Instead he found himself facing a beautiful girl dressed, for some reason, in a blue-and-white school uniform. Natsumi's black hair was tied back in a ponytail and she looked at him with something other than hostility. That was a nice change of pace.

The red streak running through her hair seemed to flicker like a flame when she bowed. "Thank you again for coming, Daisuke."

"Sure, no problem." Daisuke looked over her outfit. "Why are you dressed like that?"

"I told everyone I was going on a summer school trip. It's the best excuse I could come up with for being gone a couple of days."

"You think they believed it?"

She shrugged. "Aunt Kiyoko knows the truth, so she'll stop anyone from checking. And I am going on a trip, so it's only sort of a lie."

A pointless one, he thought, but whatever, it wasn't any of his business. "We should get moving. I'd like to wrap this up by tonight."

Natsumi nodded. "Of course. The sooner we find Dad the better."

She started off down a dirt path. At least she was wearing sneakers instead of dress shoes. He assumed they'd reach a road before too long. It wouldn't make sense to have the entry point in the middle of nowhere.

"You realize Rio might not be thrilled with us showing up given his efforts to remain hidden."

Natsumi's smile faltered. "The thought crossed my mind, but not knowing is killing me. Even if he yells and tells me to go, at least I won't be wondering anymore. Nothing else matters. My car isn't much further."

A ten-minute walk brought them to a rough backcountry road. A red convertible waited, parked on the edge.

Daisuke whistled. "Nice. After you totaled the last one, I figured you'd end up with the cheapest piece-of-crap car the clan could find."

"That wasn't my fault. There were demons on the road."

Daisuke grinned at her indignation and pulled a small

knife engraved with runes out of his pocket. The unsheathed blade glinted in the sunlight.

Natsumi eyed the knife. "What's that for?"

"The tracking spell requires a bit of blood. Yours, to be specific."

Natsumi extended her hand without a moment of hesitation. "Take what you need."

Daisuke nicked the side of her palm. When the blood welled up, he smeared it over the first inch of the knife.

"Okay, Rio, let's see where you are."

He chanted the spell and the ether responded. He spun a slow circle until he felt a tug. When he stopped, the dagger pointed directly toward Mount Fuji. Not that Rio was necessarily at the mountain.

"That way and he's pretty far off. A hundred miles at least."

Natsumi blew out a breath. "He's still alive, thank the spirits. Come on, it's about twenty miles to the highway."

They climbed into the car with Natsumi behind the wheel. Her driving could be a bit aggressive, but Daisuke didn't know his way around the area nearly as well as she did.

Besides, he was a wizard. It would take more than a car accident to kill him.

Helena tugged her sneakers on and pulled the laces tight. She'd gotten a message from the boss fifteen minutes ago calling her in to work. It wasn't a surprise. The Circle of Sorcery members tended to get short breaks if they got any breaks at all. Would she be working with Daisuke on this one or someone else? As far as she knew, none of the other members had come back from the field.

She hadn't spoken to Daisuke since the battle in Abaddon's temple and she felt kind of bad about it. Her emotions were all over the place. When she remembered what he did to Haakon—she shuddered at the image of the giant warrior exploding like a magic bomb—it twisted her up inside. It was the way he betrayed what was supposed to be at least a temporary ally that bothered her more than anything. In truth, she still hadn't made peace with what happened.

Well, she'd find out soon enough. It wasn't a long walk to the shop after all. She'd barely stood when her phone pinged. It came from Daisuke.

Gone to Japan for a couple days. Family business.

That was it. No explanation, no nothing. She frowned, perplexed. Daisuke detested most of his family and avoided any mention of them. What could compel him to visit now? Maybe whatever the boss wanted would clear things up. She wouldn't let Daisuke leave without getting more information.

Slipping the phone into her jacket pocket, Helena headed out, locking the apartment door behind her.

Her mind raced so fast she barely noticed the people walking around her. Was it strictly related to the Kugo clan or did he have a more urgent reason? She didn't know and that annoyed her.

Would it have killed him to call? As soon as the thought appeared, she winced. She'd been avoiding him, so Daisuke no doubt thought his call wouldn't have been welcome.

Why was everything so complicated?

Helena reached the alley behind Arcane Books and Trinkets a moment before Jinx came hurrying from the opposite end. The beautiful half-demon wore black slacks and a white blouse. Jinx waved when she spotted Helena and started jogging.

As soon as Jinx reached the door she asked, "Did you get Daisuke's text?"

Helena nodded. "Yeah, I got it. And I don't have a clue what's going on. He didn't call you?"

"No, though I had my phone on silent so it wouldn't wake Vixen up." Jinx smiled, showing off her slightly elongated eyeteeth. "She's getting stronger all the time. Pretty soon she'll be moving into her own place."

Helena hadn't even spoken to the ex-assassin and had no particular interest in doing so. "I assume the boss called you in too?"

"Yup. I'm kind of excited. This is the first time she's ever contacted me directly."

Jinx's excitement was equal parts cute and annoying. Helena decided not to comment and unlocked the door for them. The pair made the short walk to the boss's office.

Helena raised her fist to knock, but before her knuckles could hit the wood, the boss said, "Come in, you two."

They exchanged a quick glance then Helena pushed open the door. The boss sat behind her desk, her golden eyes glowing especially bright this morning. She gestured for them to take a seat, her expression unreadable.

As the two women settled into the guest chairs the boss said, "I'm sure you're curious about Daisuke. His uncle has gone missing and his cousin called asking for help with a tracking spell. Daisuke agreed and was well compensated for his time. He shouldn't be more than a day or two, though when you're in the field, anything can happen."

Helena let out a sigh of relief. That sounded straightforward. Daisuke told her a bit about his mission in Japan and he admitted his cousin had been helpful during the hunt for Vorgon's prison. Daisuke probably felt like he owed her one.

"So what did you call us in for?" Jinx asked.

"Before he left, Daisuke provided the location of the final two bound demons the cult of Abaddon sold. The two of you should have no trouble dealing with a couple of low-level demons and some thugs."

"You want us to work together?" Helena asked. She'd never expected to end up on a mission with her romantic rival. Though with their usual partner unavailable it made sense.

"Correct. I've spoken with a contact in Odessa's police department and they're thrilled to have some help dealing with the demon. The forces they've sent against it so far haven't fared well. I've got a jet lined up to take you there. I'm still working on Istanbul, but I should have things sorted by the time you finish in Odessa."

"When are we leaving?" Helena asked.

"As soon as you're ready. The jet is fueled and waiting at the airport."

"I'm all set," Jinx said, seeming eager to go.

Helena nodded. "I just need to grab my bag from the storeroom. Do we need to know anything else?"

"You'll be fighting a claw demon and a group of human traffickers. I doubt you'll have any real trouble, but if you need to retreat, do so. Anatoly is due back in a week and Daisuke should be here before that. No need to take unnecessary risks."

"Understood." Helena got to her feet. "Jinx, let's catch a cab to the airport."

"I could shadow walk us there," Jinx offered as she stood.

"I prefer not to show up at the airport over your shoulder like a sack of potatoes," Helena said. "It's a short drive."

"Remember to stay in touch," the boss said.

"Don't worry, Boss," Helena said. "I'm not Daisuke. Going dark is not my thing."

All three women smiled before Helena led Jinx out of the office. She paused at the storage closet long enough to grab the go bag she kept packed and ready. Once they were outside, they walked around to the front of the shop to flag down a cab.

Helena shouldered her pack. "You're not going to have a problem with me taking the lead on this job, right?"

"Of course not. I'm still very new to all of this. I wouldn't have a clue how to take the lead if you asked me to. You look surprised."

Helena hadn't realized her expression gave so much away. "I'm not, not really. It's just that you're quite a bit stronger than me. When there's a big power difference it can cause issues when the weaker party is also the senior agent. When I'm on a job with Daisuke he automatically takes over without even thinking about it."

"Does that bother you?" Jinx waved and a passing cab pulled to the curb.

Helena climbed in and when Jinx had joined her, she said, "Airport."

The cab pulled away and Helena conjured a sound barrier before answering Jinx's question. "It would bother me more if he wasn't so good at the job. Daisuke generally works alone for a reason."

"What reason?"

"He's basically stronger on his own than most of our

teams. If, heaven forbid, he ever fought the two of us, he could take us down without too much trouble."

"He would never do that." Jinx's tone rang with absolute confidence. "But speaking of agents, who's Anatoly?"

"Right, I keep forgetting you haven't met everybody. He's a Russian wizard whose ancestors had the good fortune not to be at home when World War Three started. His specialty is surveillance magic, but he's no slouch in a fight. He's been on an extended deployment to Egypt. I'm not sure what he's doing there, but he must've finished if he's coming back soon."

"What's he like?" Jinx asked.

"I don't know him that well. We've never been teamed up. The few times we chatted he was professional but distant. Not at all unusual in this line of work."

"Is it not? Everyone I've interacted with has been very friendly."

"Every agent is different. Daisuke and Carter are both ladies' men and you're definitely the sort who would catch their eye." Jinx blushed, reminding Helena once more how oddly innocent she was. "Anatoly is a widower. I've never heard of him having another relationship. But like I said, we're not close."

The cab pulled up in front of the Zurich Airport and Helena paid the cabby. The flight to Odessa wouldn't take long. Helena just hoped this mission went better than her last one without Daisuke.

CHAPTER FIVE

The convertible sped along a winding highway. Mount Fuji loomed in the distance, its snow-capped peak piercing the sky. Daisuke had cast the tracking spell again an hour ago and they were still headed in the right direction. Judging from the distance the spell indicated, Rio really was at Mount Fuji. Why he'd gone there, Daisuke couldn't begin to guess.

He glanced at Natsumi. Her white-knuckled grip on the steering wheel combined with her deep scowl made it clear she remained on edge. But at least she was obeying the speed limit. The last time he rode with her had been a life-shortening event and he was glad to avoid a repeat experience.

"How was your father acting before he left?"

Natsumi flicked a look his way before focusing on the road again. "He seemed fine, superficially at least. If you didn't know him well, you'd never guess anything was wrong. But I could tell something was... off."

"Off how?" Daisuke asked. Rio had never been the most emotionally demonstrative person and Daisuke couldn't imagine him doing anything sufficiently overt for even Natsumi to notice.

"It's hard to explain," Natsumi said, frustration evident in her voice. "It was more of a feeling I got than anything he did or said. No one else noticed anything when I asked about it."

Daisuke couldn't help wondering if it was all in her head and Rio was just off on some mission for the spirits. What that might entail he had no idea. No elemental spirit had ever spoken to him. In any case, he wasn't stupid enough to say anything given her mood.

"What about Mount Fuji?" Daisuke asked. "Anything interesting that might draw Rio?"

"It's a holy site for all of Japan." She shot him another look. "Even you should know that."

Daisuke did, in fact, know that. He didn't care, but he knew it. "I meant, something of particular interest to him."

"Not that I'm aware of. Dad was a loyal servant of the spirits, but otherwise he showed no interest in religion. Love of the clan was the closest he ever got."

That wasn't terribly helpful. Daisuke got his phone out. If Natsumi couldn't tell him anything interesting about the mountain, maybe the internet could. Lucky for him he had an upgraded browser custom made by the Circle's resident computer genius, Crystal. He tapped the icon, a circle with a lightning bolt through it, and a moment later the browser window opened.

Okay, let's see. Mount Fuji and spirit magic seemed like a good place to start.

Maybe too good. Thousands of articles popped up in response to his search. Lucky for him, the browser had a chat bot attached. He ordered it to scan and summarize the articles then set the phone in his lap. Even for a computer that would take a while.

"What are you doing?" Natsumi asked.

"Research. If I can figure out why Rio went to Mount Fuji it might give us more insight into his state of mind. I doubt he went all that way to kill himself." Natsumi made a strangled sound and Daisuke winced. Maybe that had been a little blunt. "So if that wasn't why, there has to be another reason. How far is it from the family compound to the mountain?"

"Far enough, and Dad hated driving."

"Speaking of, didn't his car have an antitheft device you could've used to track him down?"

"No, we have them all deactivated. No one wants to be traceable given what we do. What if someone hacked the system? I'm not a total idiot. I wouldn't have called you if the simple stuff was enough to find him."

Daisuke's phone beeped and he picked it up. The summary was complete. He skimmed through it, waiting for something to catch his eye. It opened with a lot of facts about pre-war religion and how the mountain played a large part in it.

An article caught his eye. Well, well, either he hadn't learned this or it wasn't common knowledge, but it seemed the elemental lords made their pact with the four human clans at a special shrine halfway up the mountain. That sounded like a promising place to look for Rio.

When he asked Natsumi about it she said, "I knew that's where the first summoning happened, but not about the shrine. Weird, that's the sort of place you'd visit on a pilgrimage. I wonder why no one ever mentioned it."

Daisuke shrugged. "I'm not the one to ask. Yoshikazu

might know, but we can't exactly call him. When we stop for gas, you should summon a spirit and ask."

"Do you think it matters?"

"Beats me, but the first rule of an investigation is to try and learn as much as you can about the target location. The odds of your father going to Mount Fuji for some other reason defies common sense. That being the case, I'd like to learn as much about the shrine as possible before we arrive."

"I guess it couldn't hurt. We're an hour from having to stop. When the time comes, I'll ask."

"Thank you." Daisuke started swiping again, but doubted he'd find anything equally interesting.

Just to cover all his bases he asked Ruq, "Have you heard anything about this place?"

"No, Master. Demons and elementals don't really get along. And by not really, I mean we don't get along at all. Abaddon will sometimes use evil fire elementals, corrupting them into proper demons, but for the most part we try our best to kill each other."

That sounded about right. He sighed and switched his phone off. There was still too much he didn't know, but pretty much every new job started that way. He'd deal with this one the same way he did all the others, one step at a time.

Natsumi glanced from the gas gauge to Daisuke and back. She was trying to be subtle, but had no doubt he was aware of every furtive look despite focusing on his phone. Natsumi had never done anything like this before and she felt kind of like a private eye from a manga. Only her fear for her father and Daisuke's deadly seriousness kept it from being fun.

The next exit was five miles away and they were down to a quarter of a tank. Time to get off and fill up. As she eased over to the inner lane, she debated what sort of spirit to contact. Obviously something strong enough to have a personality and the ability to speak. That eliminated wisps and lesser spirits. She'd always had a good rapport with fire cats. One of them should be a good option.

She hit the signal and pulled off the highway. As with pretty much every exit, a gas station waited less than a quarter mile away. She pulled into the first one they reached and stopped beside the pump.

Daisuke got out and stretched. "How worried are you about someone finding out where we are?"

"For the moment I'm not at all worried about it. Why?"

"I was going to suggest paying with cash so the transaction can't be traced, but if you're confident no one's looking for us it doesn't matter."

She'd never even considered paying cash and in fact didn't have any on her. She had a debit card that was charged with her allowance every week. She'd been saving up for a new outfit and had plenty to pay for whatever they needed, within reason.

Five minutes after they arrived, she pulled away from the pumps and parked on the side of the station. Four cars were scattered around the lot and only a handful of people were visible.

"I'll get started. Do you want me to ask the spirit about anything besides the shrine?"

Daisuke thought for a moment. "They won't tell you anything about Rio, so I guess not. I was going to check with a demon as well, but performing necromancy in a gas station parking lot isn't the best idea. Even normal people can feel the energy released when I open a hell portal."

Natsumi's lip curled in distaste. They'd all been taught since childhood that demons were evil and to be avoided at all costs. Including Daisuke, though clearly the lesson didn't take in his case. "What would demons know about an elemental shrine?"

"I can't say. Maybe a lot, maybe nothing. The point is to ask and find out."

She didn't approve and from his expression Daisuke knew she didn't approve, and it was equally clear he didn't care. Which was fair enough. Natsumi was the one asking for a favor. Complaining about his thoroughness would be rather ungrateful.

"I'm going to begin. Establishing a link and communicating through the ether should be good enough, right?"

"Yeah, no need to bring the spirit here for a simple questioning."

Natsumi shook her head. "That's completely the wrong attitude to have when dealing with spirits. It's not an interrogation, it's a chat with a friend."

He shrugged. "Whatever. Do what you have to."

She shot him a perfunctory glare and concentrated. Contacting the realm of fire was a fairly simple task for a Kugo. She thought of it like dropping by her girlfriend's house for a visit. You just had to imagine a door and knock.

Thinking of a crimson cat playing in endless flames, Natsumi raised her hand and said in Ignus, the language of the plane of fire, "Can we talk?"

The connection formed immediately and she asked, "What can you tell me about the shrine on Mount Fuji?"

"Nothing," the spirit said.

She frowned. That wasn't what she wanted to hear. "Is it where the first contract was signed between my ancestor and the lord of fire?"

"I can tell you nothing about the shrine," the spirit said.

She glanced at Daisuke who made a little slashing motion across his throat.

"I understand. Thank you for your time." The link broke and she turned to him. "That was weird. I can't imagine the spirit knew nothing."

"It didn't," Daisuke said. "You need to pay close attention to the exact words it used. 'I can tell you nothing about the shrine' isn't the same as 'I know nothing about it.' Rio probably asked them not to mention the shrine either, which is pretty close to a confirmation he's there. It's a subtle way of confirming his presence. More subtle than I expected from your father. I always thought of Rio as more of a sledge-hammer to the head sort. You learn something new every day."

Natsumi wanted to argue in her father's defense, but she had the same feeling. He always struck her as the most direct person she knew. All this cloak and dagger stuff seemed wholly out of character.

"Do you want to get back on the road or would you rather find a cemetery where you can summon your demon?"

Daisuke grinned at the jibe. "I don't need a cemetery. An unoccupied parking lot would be sufficient. The bigger question is which hell should I contact?"

"Definitely not Abaddon's," Ruq said. "You're way up at the top of his shit list."

"Best to avoid Narukami Tempest for the same reason."

Natsumi started the car and pulled onto the street while Daisuke and Ruq kept up the discussion. It kind of shocked her that he was able to talk about contacting one of the hells so casually. It probably shouldn't have, given his imp familiar.

She drove around, keeping her eyes peeled for an empty parking lot. Eventually she spotted a hardware store and drove around back to the loading docks. Sure enough, they found a big empty space with no people around.

"Will this work?" she asked.

Daisuke looked around and nodded. "Perfect. It won't take me long to check in."

He got out of the car and moved to the front, as far from the store as he could get. Daisuke raised his arms and the temperature dropped fifteen degrees. Darkness gathered around him and it felt like the day the demon prison opened, though less intense. He chanted in a language that set her teeth on edge.

"You need to toughen up." Natsumi nearly jumped out of her skin when the imp spoke right beside her ear. "If this tiny amount of corruption is enough to bother you, there's no way you'll make it as a Circle agent."

Before she could speak, a black disk about the size of her head appeared in midair. He said something in the same language as the spell.

"He's asking about the shrine," Ruq said. "Sounds like a divine barrier keeps demons away. That could be a problem for me. The demon has no information about the shrine."

The disk vanished and Daisuke got back in the car.

"No luck, huh?" she asked.

"Did Ruq translate for you?"

"Yeah, he said the barrier might be a problem for him."

Daisuke clicked his seatbelt. "Maybe, but I doubt it. From the sounds of it, the barrier is designed to block the forces of Hell from seeing the mountain. I didn't get the impression it was an actual forbiddance."

"Blocking the whole mountain would be a huge task," Ruq said. "Even a viewing barrier that big is impressive. I wonder how they did it."

Daisuke shook his head. "Irrelevant for our purposes. As long as it doesn't stop us from reaching Rio, nothing else matters."

Natsumi wholeheartedly agreed with his sentiment. She pulled out of the parking lot and turned toward the highway more determined than ever to find her father.

CHAPTER SIX

T he Circle's jet raced through the clouds toward Odessa. Helena and Jinx had no trouble boarding in Zurich and fifteen minutes later they were in the air. Helena wished they had more details about the targets but she was confident they could handle one demon and some guys with guns.

Jinx sat across from her, peering out the small oval window at the patchwork landscape far below. The beautiful half-demon had seemed on edge since they took off. Maybe she was nervous about being on a mission without Daisuke for the first time. Helena couldn't deny she was far less powerful than him, but she was still confident they could handle the mission.

"You okay?" Helena finally asked.

"Yeah, fine." Jinx looked away from the window. "Do you think it will be easy? Just swoop in, kill the demon, and leave?"

"Based on our intel, it should be. But when it comes to fieldwork, nothing is guaranteed. I imagine Daisuke told you all about that when you were looking for the Devil Man."

"He did, and he was right. I hope things go more smoothly today."

Helena hoped so too. The last thing she wanted was to wind up locked in a cell without access to her magic. If she never had to experience that again it would suit her fine.

"Don't worry, we'll be okay. One measly demon doesn't stand a chance against us." Helena flashed a smile she hoped would put Jinx at ease. While she might not be best friends with the woman, they were partners on this mission and fellow Circle members. Helena would do her best for Jinx and was confident Jinx would return the favor.

The plane began its descent, passing through the clouds to reveal the sprawling city of Odessa below, all gray concrete and asphalt. The city was close enough to Russia that it ended up badly damaged during World War Three and had to be almost completely rebuilt. Pity it had been done with an eye for speed rather than beauty.

And speaking of beauty, the Black Sea glittered to their right. A gorgeous expanse of blue that stretched as far as she could see to the horizon.

A familiar tingle of anticipation mixed with wariness ran through her. No matter how routine, every mission held the potential for deadly surprises. Part of her relished the excitement even as the rational part recognized an ugly death may well await her.

The plane jolted and the tires shrieked when they hit the landing strip. They gradually slowed and began to taxi over to the terminal. Private planes had their own area and soon enough they rolled to a stop.

The pilot's voice came over the intercom. "We have

landed safely at Odessa International Airport. We will refuel and be ready to go in twenty-four hours."

If things went well, they shouldn't need more than that. Helena undid her seatbelt and stood. Jinx joined her a moment later and the two women made their way to the exit where the stewardess had the door open.

Five steps brought them onto the tarmac. A swirling wind whipped Helena's blond hair across her face. She pushed it back and scanned the area, spotting a stern-faced man in a gray suit striding toward them. This guy had to be the police liaison.

"I'm Sergeant Rostolov," he said in accented but still understandable English. He thrust out a hand. "The Odessa PD thanks you for your help in resolving this matter. Please, the car is waiting."

He gestured to an unmarked black sedan idling nearby before marching back toward it. Helena fell in beside him and Jinx brought up the rear. A couple minutes later they pulled away from the airport with Rostolov at the wheel.

"What's the situation, Sergeant?" Helena asked.

Rostolov kept his eyes on the road as he guided the car through busy streets. "It's a damned mess. We sent two teams in to deal with them and their damn monster shredded both, the wizards included. Since they seem content to keep their business to the waterfront, the powers that be decided to only observe them for now. They haven't bothered our look-outs. Our powerlessness seems to amuse the bastards."

"We're likely going to have to kill a bunch of criminals to do this successfully. Will that be a problem?" Helena wasn't as indifferent to killing as Daisuke, but she'd been at this long enough to understand it couldn't be avoided sometimes and this looked like one of those times.

"No, ma'am. Whatever force you need to use is acceptable to eliminate that demon. If a few scumbag criminals end up caught in the crossfire, no one will complain. If you can avoid the civilians with any stray spells, that would be ideal."

"Of course, we're here to protect the citizens, not harm them."

The car rolled to a stop within sight of a row of sprawling warehouses running along the docks. Three huge ships were busy getting unloaded by giant cranes while men in hard hats rushed around.

"Everything looks normal," Jinx said.

"It is, sort of." Rostolov killed the engine and turned to face the two women. "They let business continue, but they're taking a cut off the top from the shipping companies. It's easy money for them. A week of continuous observation has given us a pretty good idea of the shape of their operation. The only thing we haven't figured out is where they keep the people they're trafficking. Spotters have reported seeing no sign of them."

"Okay, thanks. We'll take it from here. Have your people move in as soon as we destroy the demon." Helena slid out of the car and Jinx joined her. "I can sense it from here."

"Me too," Jinx said. "And something else, out in the water. Not sure what, but it has a different flavor of corruption than the closer one."

Helena frowned and shifted her gaze out over the Black Sea. She couldn't sense anything. Maybe Jinx had a longer range than her. "As long as whatever's out there stays out there, I don't care. Let's see what we can do."

Before Helena could take a step, Rostolov rolled down his window and held out a blocky radio. "Just in case."

JAMES E. WISHER

She clipped the radio to her belt and nodded before setting out toward the source of corruption.

When they'd put some distance between themselves and Rostolov, Jinx asked, "Do you want me to send some shadows in first to scout it out?"

"No need," Helena said. "Finding the demon won't be a problem, but keep those shadows ready. If any trigger-happy goons try to stop us, take them out."

"Do you want them alive?"

Helena stopped. "You can do that?"

"Sure, I stopped some muggers for Daisuke in the Sty and didn't kill any of them."

"That would be ideal. Thank you."

Jinx's smile was adorable. Her red eyes flashed and the temperature dropped a few degrees. "They're ready."

The two of them strode down the bustling docks. The area hummed with activity. On either side, workers hauled crates and forklifts beeped as they backed up. It was so strange seeing all this while a demon was only yards away.

Maybe it was a way to prevent the authorities from trying again with more powerful magic. So many potential casualties would make them think twice.

The corrupt presence drew her unerringly to the central warehouse, a hulking monstrosity of corrugated metal. No people were immediately visible, but she could sense about twenty human life forces inside with the demon.

They were only a few paces from the warehouse entrance when a sudden surge of corruption from the sea brought Helena to a dead stop.

"It's coming," Jinx said.

Before Helena could respond, an ear-splitting roar shook the air. Massive tentacles, slick with brine and writhing with

38

unholy power, burst from the water. They smashed into the docks, splintering wood and sending people and cargo flying like rag dolls.

Screams of terror filled the air and people ran toward the city as fast as they could.

The warehouse doors slammed outward as the claw demon emerged, its crimson skin glistening and bladed hands dripping with hellfire. It raced toward the colossal octopus, blades slashing at its tentacles.

Helena had been so distracted by the demons that only now did she notice the men who emerged from the warehouse.

"Jinx!" Helena shouted over the roars, and pointed at the men. "Get them!"

Jinx narrowed her eyes and dark shapes surged toward the criminals.

Trusting Jinx to handle the thugs, Helena raised a golden barrier that deflected incoming debris, shielding both them and the fleeing civilians.

Meanwhile, the dueling demons tore into each other, the claw demon's blades ripping through rubbery flesh as the octopus's tentacles sought to crush it.

Helena wanted no part of that fight. She'd deal with whichever survived.

The battle dragged on. Two tentacles had been severed from the octopus while one of the claw demon's arms was bent in the wrong direction. Helena couldn't tell which, if either, was winning.

As if in answer to her unspoken question, the octopus smashed the claw demon through the side of one of the warehouses before retreating beneath the waves.

"Now's our chance!" Helena shifted her magic from

defense to offense, blasting the claw demon with lances of golden energy as it tried to climb out of the building.

Jinx joined in, inky black flames splashing across the demon's body. In moments it was reduced to a rapidly dissolving puddle of black goo.

She didn't even have a chance to use the radio Rostolov provided before wailing sirens appeared in the distance. Soon, the docks were swarming with police cars and ambulances.

Helena motioned Jinx over beside the unconscious criminals. None of the men so much as flinched.

It wasn't long before Rostolov hurried over to join them, his brow furrowed with worry. "The octopus... Where the hell did it come from?"

Helena shook her head. "I can't say for certain, but it was definitely demonic in nature. If I had to guess, I'd say your criminals got on the bad side of a demon cult."

"Most likely Dagon's," Jinx said. "A giant demonic octopus fits his aesthetic perfectly."

Helena should've thought of that. Since Dagon didn't participate in the battle with Solomon the Wise, they seldom encountered his cult on their missions.

Pity that had to change today.

Rostolov had gone pale, his eyes so wide the whites were visible all around the pupil. "Will it come back?"

Helena shook her head. "Impossible to say. You need to figure out why it attacked in the first place. Your prisoners might be able to tell you something when they wake up."

"Please, you must stay. We can't deal with something like this on our own. That thing looked even stronger than the other demon."

"It was," Jinx said. "About twenty percent stronger."

Rostolov gaped at her.

Helena patted his shoulder. "I need to call my boss, but if she agrees, we'll do our best to help. I'll need full access to the prisoners and the warehouse. There can't be any secrets if we're going to figure this out."

Rostolov sagged and Helena feared he might faint. "Thank you. Whatever you need, I'll see that you have it."

Helena smiled in a way he hopefully found reassuring and motioned Jinx further away.

"This is a little more than we planned on," Jinx said.

"You have a gift for understatement. I need to call the boss. Keep an eye on things for me?"

"Sure, no problem." Jinx let out a little sigh. "I wish Daisuke was here."

Helena said nothing as she dialed, but she wished he was too.

CHAPTER SEVEN

I t was late in the afternoon when Daisuke and Natsumi reached the parking lot at the base of Mount Fuji. A dozen cars filled half the lot. She parked the convertible next to a little hatchback that reminded him of her old car. A couple of families were loading their kids into an SUV a few spots away. Not wanting to scare anyone, Daisuke stayed in the car to check the tracking spell.

He pulled out the dagger stained with Natsumi's blood, channeled ether into the blade, and pointed it toward the mountain. Sure enough, when he angled it up it locked on to a spot about halfway to the top.

"He's there, no doubt about it."

"What in the world could've brought my father here?"

Daisuke shook his head and put the knife away. He wouldn't have been able to guess what Rio was thinking at the best of times and he certainly couldn't now.

"Why don't we go ask him?"

"Right!" Natsumi hopped out of the car and Daisuke joined her.

As soon as he closed the door, she locked it and set out at a determined march toward the trailhead. To one side of the dirt path sat a weathered ranger station. It wasn't much more than a shack with a window on the side. A middle-aged man in a park service uniform looked up from some paperwork as they approached.

"Can I help you folks?" the ranger asked. "Getting pretty late to start up the trail. You'll have to hurry to reach the first campsite before dark."

"I appreciate the warning," Daisuke said. "While we're here we were looking forward to visiting the elemental shrine. Could you tell us how far up it is?"

The ranger's brow furrowed. "Elemental shrine? I'm sorry, son, but there's no shrine on Mount Fuji. Are you sure you have the right mountain?"

Daisuke stared for a moment. Did this guy seriously think he mistook Mount Fuji for somewhere else? It couldn't be hot enough in that shack to melt his brain, so that wasn't the problem. Not wanting to cause a scene he said, "Perhaps I did. Thank you for your time."

When they'd put some distance between themselves and the shack Natsumi asked, "What mountain do you think he was talking about?"

"I have no idea and I doubt he does either. Some magic must be obscuring knowledge of the shrine. If he's been working here for as long as it looks like, the spell has likely scrambled his brain."

"I never heard of magic like that," Natsumi said.

"That makes two of us. Between the blocking magic on the mountain and now this, something major must be going on."

"Ardent Lilly's followers are good at this sort of thing,"

Ruq said.

Natsumi glared in the direction of Ruq's voice. "My father did not come to visit a demon cult."

"Knock it off, both of you. I'm sure Rio didn't intentionally visit a demon cult, but he might've been deceived. This may end up being a trap. Though to be fair I've half been expecting one since I arrived."

"Really?" Natsumi asked.

"Yes, really. In this line of work you seldom go wrong when you assume the worst. The main thing is, Rio is close and alive. If he's fine, great. If he needs rescuing, well, killing evil people is what I do. Saving your father in the process would be a nice bonus."

Natsumi shot him another look but made no further comments.

They set off up the well-maintained trail at a brisk clip, Daisuke's long legs eating up the distance. Hikers descended the path as people called it a day. They passed families with young children meandering along as well as serious athletes outfitted in high-tech climbing gear training for more strenuous peaks.

Every half hour, when no other people were in sight, Daisuke paused to check the tracking spell. Each time, the pulse of ether confirmed they were drawing closer to their target. The sun was getting lower all the time and soon it would be totally dark.

Daisuke stopped, eyeing a row of small cabins off to one side of the trail. They'd been built to provide shelter for climbers wanting to camp out. That was going to be them in short order.

"It'll be dark soon," he said. "Maybe we should stop for the night and make an early start in the morning."

"No way," Natsumi said. "We're so close now, I can feel it. I'm not stopping until we find Dad."

Daisuke sighed but didn't argue. He'd expected that reaction in any case. "Okay, we keep going. Maybe we'll luck out and find him before one of us trips and breaks an ankle."

As dusk deepened into full night, the stars began to appear overhead. When the time came to check the tracking spell again, Daisuke frowned. The pull that had been steadily growing stronger as they climbed had gotten weaker.

"What's going on now?" he muttered.

Natsumi glanced over. "What's wrong?"

"It's weird. The spell's acting like we've gone too far, but we didn't pass him or anything which might serve as a hiding place. We must have missed something. Come on, we're going back. I'll keep the dagger out this time to see if I can get a more precise fix on Rio's location. It's not like anyone's going to see it in the dark."

Natsumi conjured a ball of fire to light the path. "Better?"

He ignored her sarcastic tone and said, "Yes, thank you."

They backtracked down the trail, Daisuke holding the knife like a dowsing rod. The tug grew stronger again, pulling him along.

Then it turned toward a sheer cliff face.

Daisuke stopped dead in the middle of the path, the knife quivering in his grip as it pointed at the solid stone of the mountainside. "He's beyond the wall, about two hundred yards straight through the rock."

"Are you sure?" Natsumi stared at the cliff face. "It's solid stone."

"Maybe, maybe not." Daisuke placed his free hand against the rock wall. The surface was cool, rough, and firm. A faint tingle ran through his palm. "Hmm."

Daisuke sent a pulse of ether into the stone. Like sonar, the burst of energy echoed back, revealing a hidden space beyond.

"There's a tunnel hidden behind about six inches of rock. What do you want to bet it leads to the shrine?"

Natsumi shook her head. "How do we get in?"

"That, at least, is easy enough." Daisuke stepped back and drew a symbol in the air before charging it with ether. He snapped his fingers and the rock shattered like glass to reveal the mouth of a tunnel. A stride beyond the entrance, someone had forged a glowing rune that seemed to be the source of the ward hiding the shrine from magical detection. "There we are."

Natsumi sent her conjured flame ahead to light their path. "Let's go."

The tunnel stretched onward, but Daisuke could just barely see a light at the end. It didn't look much bigger than a quarter but at least he was confident the tunnel had an exit.

"Want me to take a look?" Ruq asked.

"No," Daisuke said. "We stick together until we figure out what we're dealing with."

They kept going, slow and steady. Natsumi's conjured flame cast a flickering glow upon the rough-hewn walls. It looked like someone had dug the tunnel out rather than using magic to form it. The air was chill and damp with a strange, musty scent lying over everything.

Around two hundred yards in, the tunnel opened into a cavern that stole his breath. Glowing crystals studded the walls and ceiling. They pulsed with a gentle light that soothed his nerves. Ponds with fountains dotted the landscape, connected by narrow brooks. Last but far from least were four white marble temples that would've looked more at home in Greece than Japan. One rested at each of the cardinal directions.

"This has to be the elemental shrine," Daisuke said. "It's... something."

Natsumi had her gaze locked on a lone figure seated in the center of an intricate spell circle. "Dad!"

Before Daisuke could offer a word of warning, she sprinted toward him, feet flying over an ornate bridge that spanned one of the brooks. At least she had sense enough to stop at the edge of the circle.

Daisuke followed at a more sedate pace.

"Natsumi." Rio stood, his movements stiff and pained. He was clearly still suffering from the effects of the battle with Haakon. As he turned to face them, he shifted his right arm.

Natsumi gasped and Daisuke didn't blame her. From the elbow down, a skeletal forearm and hand had regrown. As they watched, fine strands of muscle wove themselves over the bare framework.

"How?" Natsumi asked.

Rio met her gaze, completely ignoring Daisuke in the process. "I received a message from a wizard who offered to heal my arm. In exchange I had to leave at once and tell no one where I was going. I even had to forbid the spirits from revealing my location."

Daisuke frowned. None of this made any sense. Why would any wizard make such an offer? Most wizards were far from altruistic.

Before he could speak, Natsumi gave voice to the question in Daisuke's mind. "What was the point of all that?"

Rio shifted his gaze to Daisuke. "He wanted to draw you here, Daisuke. To meet you. When the spirits refused her, we figured Natsumi would contact you for help. No wizard in

Japan would take the job without my brother's approval and Yoshikazu would never defy the will of the spirits."

"And it worked beautifully." A man approached from the opposite direction. He moved so silently Daisuke hadn't heard a thing. Even his life force was masked.

The man, the wizard to be more precise, came closer. He did nothing threatening, though Daisuke never lowered his guard.

The stranger was tall, conventionally handsome, probably European, with a chiseled jawline, brown hair, and powerful build partially hidden by a traditional black kimono. "Welcome, Daisuke. It's good to finally meet you."

"You have my attention." He kept his voice even and calm. "You also have me at a disadvantage. I don't even know your name."

The wizard smiled, flashing straight white teeth. "My name is Miles Bartlett, though I'm sure that means nothing to you. I've been waiting a long time for this meeting."

"You could've just sent a text. There's no need for all this cloak-and-dagger bullshit."

"On the contrary, it's very much needed. Let's give father and daughter a few minutes alone. Some of what I have to say is best kept between us. Come along."

Much as he disliked the highhanded treatment, Daisuke's curiosity compelled him to follow. Hopefully he'd like what he heard.

CHAPTER EIGHT

Miles led Daisuke away from the spell circle where Rio and Natsumi were chatting. They crossed one of the bridges and turned toward a temple. At the steps Miles stopped and sat facing him. Daisuke frowned but sat as well. Ruq appeared in his lap in rat form and Daisuke absently scratched his head. This whole situation struck him as far too casual, but whatever.

"Why don't we go inside?" Daisuke asked.

"There's nowhere to sit inside."

"Okay, what's so bloody important you had to trick me into coming all the way here?"

"Did your mother tell you anything about your father?" Miles asked.

Daisuke stared at him in disbelief. "You've got to be shitting me. You?"

Miles nodded. "Hello, son. Though it may be twenty-two years too late, I am pleased to meet you. I've been watching your growth as a wizard with great interest. I must say, even

49

for one of the blood, you have shown tremendous potential. Out of all my children, you're by far the strongest."

Daisuke was having trouble processing the news. Even knowing his biological father was out there somewhere, he never expected to meet the man, much less like this.

"I'm sure you have questions," Miles said. "I'll do my best to answer them."

"Okay, here's the most important one. What do you want?"

Now it was Miles's turn to be taken back. "That's your first question? Not, where have I been or something about your brothers and sisters?"

Daisuke shrugged. "It's hard to care about strangers. But it's very easy to care about how you're trying to manipulate me. So?"

Miles sighed. "I knew you weren't going to be excited about my sudden appearance, but I didn't think you were going to be quite this indifferent. It's difficult to answer your question without giving you a bit of background. So, if you don't mind, I'd like to tell you everything from the beginning."

Daisuke shrugged. "Go for it. I'm all ears."

"Before I revealed myself, I needed to confirm that you weren't willing to join Solomon the Great. I was fairly confident, but when you killed Haakon and Vanessa, I knew for sure you were the partner I needed."

"I'm not much of a joiner and I'm already a member of the Circle of Sorcery. What, exactly, is it you need my help to do?"

"I need you to help me kill my brother before he does something that will leave the world in darkness for all eternity at best and completely destroyed at worst."

Daisuke rubbed the bridge of his nose. He had a bad feeling about this. "Who's your brother?"

"Solomon the Great. He's also your uncle, obviously, though I doubt he's aware of it. His real name is Solomon Bartlett and he's two years older than me. I'm not sure when it happened, but at some point he became obsessed with the legend of Solomon the Wise. Eventually he started to believe he was the ancient wizard's reincarnation and that it was his duty to bring order to the world with himself as supreme ruler."

"Ruling the world and trying to destroy it are two very different things," Daisuke said. "Granted neither of them are good, but they're still different."

"No, they're not," Miles said. "A world ruled by an insane wizard using the power of demons is about as dark as it gets and if the seventy-two should break free of his control, think of the damage they might do. Earth would be transformed into a Hell World. It would be a planetary version of what almost happened in Kurisato. The lords of Hell would go to war to control our world with humanity caught in the middle. Should Heaven decide to join the fight it would be even worse. If you doubt me, ask your friend Angelique."

Daisuke frowned. "You've met the boss?"

"No, but I know what she is. As I said, I've been following your growth with great interest."

Daisuke got up and paced around. His head was spinning. He couldn't make such an important decision at the drop of a hat.

He turned back and asked, "How many kids do you have?"

Miles's brow furrowed as he considered. "A couple hundred, maybe. I made sure to impregnate any woman I encountered who was of the blood. Honestly, the results have been very disappointing. Less than ten percent ended up being wizards and only five, including you, were strong enough to be of any use in the fight that's coming. One of the greatest ironies of this entire situation is that my brother's second-in -command is your elder half sister."

"Let me get this straight. My mom is of the blood? She's not even a wizard."

"Most of those descended from Solomon the Wise aren't. It's a very recessive trait. However, when it expresses itself strongly, the results are amazing. That's why I made sure to have as many kids as possible. It's simply a numbers' game."

Daisuke didn't like his attitude toward his many children, but in the end it wasn't relevant to the current situation. "Okay, so you approached me. One of your more capable daughters is with the other team. That leaves three strong ones. What have you done about them?"

"Nothing particularly promising. Grant was especially bitter about what he saw as my abandonment and immediately rejected my suggestion of joining forces. He even went so far as to threaten to kill me should I ever approach him again. A very immature reaction given the threat we're all facing."

"Yeah, but also very understandable. When you were running around knocking up every chick you could find with the right bloodline, did it not occur to you that this was the reaction you'd get should you show up again out of the blue?"

Miles frowned. "I hadn't thought about it. Any rational person should be able to set aside such a minor consideration for the good of the world."

"Wow, okay. I can see you're a powerful wizard, but

you're clearly clueless about people if you expected a rational reaction from a kid you abandoned."

"You seem to be handling it pretty well."

Daisuke's laugh was humorless. "I've had practice. It took me most of eight years to stop hating Yoshikazu and that only got me to indifference. Hating a stranger is harder. I started at indifference with you. What about the other two?"

"Melissa wasn't interested either. She's doing aid work in Africa, using her magic to heal the desperately sick. While she wasn't angry with me, she refused to quit her mission. As for Zahra, she's the power behind the throne of Iran and had no interest in leaving the palace. Most depressingly, Tatiana was recruited by Solomon before I could reach her. She would no doubt be happy to kill me should the opportunity arise. You're my last hope."

"It seems like our interests align. I won't leave the Circle, but I see no reason we can't work together when necessary. Killing Solomon the Great would please my boss no end, so I doubt she'll complain. You understand I'm going to tell her everything?"

"By all means do what you think best. We're well past the point of secrets among allies having any value."

"Swell. One last question then I need to find somewhere to sleep. Do you know where to find Solomon?"

Miles let out another long sigh. "Unfortunately, I do not. He's found some way to hide himself and he seldom emerges. However, now that I have an ally in you, finding my brother is my top priority. I'll be abandoning this location as soon as Rio completes his healing."

Daisuke yawned, disappointed but hardly surprised by Miles's answer. "I'll give you my cellphone number before I leave in the morning. If you need me again, send a text."

W hen Daisuke had gone off to talk with the strange wizard who was responsible for bringing them all here, Natsumi focused on her father. She tried not to stare at his slowly regenerating arm, but it was difficult to look away.

"I'm sorry I worried you." He bowed low.

Natsumi sighed. "It's fine, I guess. Getting your arm back is a pretty big deal. If the price was a little worry from me and a little of Daisuke's time, it's worth it. Just out of curiosity, what was plan B if I didn't call him?"

"If Miles had a backup plan, he didn't share it with me. In fact, he barely spoke to me after I arrived and he activated the spell. I won't be going back with you tomorrow. The magic requires me to stay here until it's complete. Best-case scenario, I'll be home in another week."

Natsumi wasn't thrilled about that, but she nodded. "I'd like to stay, but I can't be gone for that long. I already disobeyed Uncle Yoshikazu to come looking for you. If I stayed away for a week, I fear he wouldn't take it well."

"My brother isn't the violent sort, so I doubt he'd hurt you, but you can be sure he would be slow to trust you with any important family assignments. It will help your cause if you tell him everything when you get home."

"If you think that's best, I will." Natsumi indicated his damaged arm. "Does it hurt?"

"No, it itches more than anything. Like ants are crawling all over my arm. I can't say the sensation is pleasant, but I didn't imagine regrowing a limb would be. If this restores me to full strength, it'll be worth the price. I dislike feeling useless."

She took a step closer. "You were never useless. Don't talk about yourself that way."

A faint smile appeared, a rare sight on her father's normally stern face. "Even I can't help how I feel, but I do appreciate your concern."

"With Mom gone, you're all I have left. Of course I'm concerned." Hoping to lighten the mood she asked, "Where's your car?"

"In a parking garage a mile from here."

Natsumi grinned. "I wish I could see the look on the ranger's face when you come back down with a new arm."

"I'll leave under an invisibility spell. That's a conversation I'd prefer to avoid."

"I bet." Natsumi yawned. Now that the fear had gone, exhaustion had replaced it. "I'm going to find Daisuke and see if there's somewhere around here we can sleep. See you in the morning."

"Before you lie down, be sure to visit the fire temple and pay your respects to the spirits."

Natsumi hadn't even thought about that but said, "I will."

Her father settled back down and she strode off to find Daisuke. Despite being huge for a cavern, it still wasn't that large of a space. She spotted him sitting on the steps of the fire temple. That was convenient for her. Of their host she saw no sign. It seemed the two men had concluded their discussion.

He looked up at her approach. "Hey. How's Rio?"

"Dad's fine, maybe a little embarrassed that he caused so much fuss." She sat beside him. "If there's one thing he dislikes, it's fuss. He says he has to hang around here for another week or so to finish healing."

Daisuke nodded. "Are you staying or going?"

"I can't stay here for a week. Thanks again for helping me find him."

"Sure, no sweat. I got some interesting intel as well, so all's well that ends well. Miles says we can camp out anywhere we want. The grass looks softer than the ground in the Outback at least."

"Do you mind sharing what he told you?" Natsumi asked.

"No, but I wouldn't recommend you telling anyone else."

Daisuke told her everything and by the end Natsumi's jaw was hanging loose. "He's your father?!"

"Would you shut up?" Daisuke looked back at her dad and Natsumi winced.

"Sorry. Anyway, I thought you didn't care what the clan thought of you."

"I don't, but I'd prefer not to cause Mom a bunch of trouble."

Natsumi was ashamed to admit she hadn't even thought about what might happen to Aunt Kiyoko if the clan found out about Daisuke's true parentage. Even if it happened before the marriage and wasn't technically an affair it would still make things awkward at best.

"So you trust him enough to work with him? I would've thought you'd be more hesitant."

"I'm plenty hesitant, but he wants Solomon the Great dead as much as I do. I'll work with him to the extent our interests align. And if he tries to betray me, I'll make him regret his decision."

Daisuke said that in the coldest, calmest tone she'd ever heard. Natsumi truly believed in that moment he could've cut Miles's throat without blinking an eye.

"I need to pay my respects to the fire spirits. Want to join me?"

"The spirits made their feelings about me clear. I doubt I'd be welcome in their temple."

"Do you know why?" Natsumi asked. "Maybe they wouldn't give their blessing to someone outside the clan, but that doesn't mean they automatically hate you."

He shrugged. "I've always been rubbish at spirit magic, so I saw no reason to worry about it."

"Maybe now's a good time to find out." Natsumi got to her feet and yanked Daisuke to his, spilling Ruq out of his lap.

"Hey!" the imp complained as he righted himself.

"Come on." She held on to his hand and dragged him up the steps to the entrance of the fire temple. He pulled back but not with any real effort.

No door blocked the entrance so she pulled him right in. The interior wasn't anything overwhelming. It was an empty white stone room with an obsidian altar in the center. Nothing reacted as the two of them crossed the open space and stopped in front of the altar.

Natsumi finally let go of his hand, pressed her palms together, and bowed. "Oh king of fire, your humble servant offers her greetings."

For a moment she thought her prayer was going to be ignored but then the temperature rose and a massive, blazing fire roared out of the altar. It shot so high it nearly touched the ceiling. From the center of the flames a deep voice boomed. "Welcome to our temple, child of Kugo. Your prayer is gratefully accepted."

Natsumi's knees trembled. This overwhelming presence had to be the fire king himself. "May I be permitted a question?"

"All is permitted a beloved child," the fire king said.

"Why did you deny Daisuke your blessing?"

"He is not of Kugo blood."

"So you let an innocent child be burned and cast out like a criminal?" She tried to keep her anger in check, but it felt so wrong. The more she thought about it the more she realized none of what happened was Daisuke's fault. He'd been a victim. "How is that fair?"

"Natsumi…" Daisuke's voice carried a hint of warning but she ignored it. She was going to find out the truth and damn the consequences.

"Fairness has no bearing on anything," the fire king said. "Only the contract matters. Those of Kugo blood will receive our blessing. Those who marry into the clan will receive our protection. That was the agreement. No more and no less. We have honored the bargain for many of your generations and we will continue to honor it for as long as the Kugo clan exists."

"Hating him because he's not a Kugo is wrong," Natsumi said.

"While we do not love the boy, neither do we hate him," the fire king said. "He hates us and it blocks him from mastering spirit magic. That is all."

The fire vanished and Natsumi turned to face Daisuke. He had a conflicted expression and seemed deep in thought.

"Is that true?" she asked. "Do you hate the spirits?"

"Yes, though I thought it was mutual. Somehow being disregarded completely feels even worse than being hated." He shrugged and she wanted to shake him. "I'm going to find a nice soft patch of grass to sleep on. You want to keep praying or get some shuteye?"

She gave him one last searching look then said, "It's sleep

for me. I'd like to leave before the trail gets too crowded in the morning."

CHAPTER NINE

Helena held the phone to her ear while surveying the chaotic scene at the warehouse. Sirens wailed as ambulances and police cars crowded the docks. Paramedics rushed to help the injured, while officers handcuffed dazed gang members. The acrid smell of smoke and brimstone lingered in the air. The cacophony made it nearly impossible to hear the boss.

"Where's the octopus now?" the boss asked.

"I don't know," Helena said. "It swam away after the claw demon cut a couple of its tentacles off. The local police want Jinx and me to stay and help track it down. You said we're supposed to head to Istanbul, but honestly, Sergeant Rostolov is out of his league. It's your call, but I'd like to try and sort things out before we leave."

"I agree," the boss said. "I've heard nothing about the cult of Dagon being active in the Black Sea area. Assuming Jinx is right about the source of the attack, and I'm confident she is, there might be some new threat brewing. Do what you can.

I'll send Anatoly to Istanbul to survey the situation. Keep me informed."

"I will." Helena hesitated then asked, "Have you heard from Daisuke?"

"Not yet, but it hasn't even been a day. He can take care of himself. You need to worry about your own situation. Take care."

The line went dead and she slipped the phone into her pocket. She caught Jinx's eye and waved her closer.

"What did she say?" Jinx asked.

"We're staying. Anatoly's stuck with Istanbul, observation only for now."

"That's good. I think Sergeant Rostolov might've had a heart attack if we left him to handle this on his own."

Helena smiled. "I think you might be right. Let's find him and break the good news."

They found him near the warehouse entrance, barking orders in Ukrainian while gesturing at the pile of unconscious criminals. As the women approached, Rostolov focused on them. He was chewing the side of his lip though he seemed unaware of it.

"We'll be imposing on your hospitality for a little longer, Sergeant."

"Thank heaven for that. Where do you want to start? Anything you need, just ask. We're at your disposal."

Helena's gaze drifted to the unconscious gang members being loaded into ambulances, their faces pale and twisted from their encounter with Jinx's shadows. "Doesn't look like this lot will be waking up anytime soon. Let's take a closer look at the warehouse."

Rostolov led them into the massive building where officers were methodically searching through stacks of crates and containers. Helena glanced at the contents of one and shook her head. A two-hundred-pound wheel of cheese was pretty far from her expectations for a human trafficking operation.

"Do you need me to clear the area so you can…" Rostolov wiggled his fingers.

Helena smiled at his discomfort. "No need, Sergeant. Your team can keep working. Jinx, let's see what we can find. I'll go right, you go left."

Helena concentrated and sent ether out in every direction. The detection spell was a simple one, but very effective for covering a large area. Tendrils of magic snaked through the air, probing every corner and crevice for anything.

After a few minutes of searching, Helena stiffened. Tunnels ran beneath the warehouse. She gave them a closer look. They weren't natural, that was for sure. The passages were made of smooth concrete. There was no way to tell how long they'd been there, but given the lack of wear she guessed not too long.

"Jinx, did you find anything?" Helena asked.

"Not yet. You?"

"There are some tunnels over here. Help me find the entrance."

Jinx hurried over and the two women began scanning the floor. Helena traced the tunnels and soon took a knee beside a nearly invisible seam. If she hadn't known about the tunnels, she never would've spotted it.

"Bingo," Helena said. "Would you send a shadow down for a closer look?"

A humanoid shape detached itself from Jinx's shadow and sank into the floor. It hadn't been gone any time before Jinx said, "There's a barrier. It can't pass through."

"A barrier? I didn't think these clowns had a wizard on staff. At least I saw no sign of one during the battle. We'll have to take a closer look." Helena straightened and waved to draw Rostolov's attention.

The good sergeant hurried over. "Yes, ma'am?"

"We found a trapdoor connected to some tunnels. Could I trouble you for a couple of guys with crowbars?"

He hesitated, looking from her to the floor and back.

"It's safe," Helena said. "I want to save my strength in case there's a fight."

"Right, sorry." Rostolov bellowed an order and two burly cops came over, crowbars in hand.

Helena pointed out the edge of the trapdoor and they got to work. The process didn't take long and soon they were levering the heavy stone door open. Hydraulic pistons on either side no doubt gave the smugglers easier access. Someone must've had a remote to activate them.

The cops backed away and Helena peered into the darkness. Iron rungs hammered into the cement acted like a ladder. She conjured a small golden light which flew into the dark. Soon enough it hit the barrier and winked out of existence.

"Looks like more of a generalized anti-magic barrier than a spirit barrier. What a pain." She turned to Rostolov. "Could I trouble you for a flashlight?"

One of the crowbar guys responded first, pulling a heavy-duty flashlight out of the holster on his belt and handing it to her with a wink. Not in the mood to flirt, she took the light and hopped down the opening. An effort of will slowed her descent and she landed lightly on the floor. A moment later Jinx appeared beside her.

When she snapped the light on, all it revealed was an

ordinary square tunnel. A bit of condensation had gathered on the walls but that was it.

About twenty yards in they reached the barrier. It was a faint shimmering in the ether. Nothing about it looked dangerous, but Helena approached with all her defenses primed.

She poked a finger through it. No discomfort, but it did negate all her spells.

Steeling herself, Helena took a step. And emerged unscathed on the other side. As she thought, it was safe. When Jinx joined her, the woman winced.

"You okay?" Helena asked.

"That stung a bit, but nothing serious. Now that I'm through it's fine. Let's keep going."

Helena turned back up the tunnel. Out of curiosity she activated a basic shield spell and found it worked fine. Magic couldn't pass through but worked normally on either side. She couldn't remember encountering a barrier like this one before.

Right, she could be fascinated later. They had a job to finish.

Her flashlight cast eerie shadows on the damp walls as they made their way deeper underground. Their footsteps echoed in the silence. The steady, hollow thunks put Helena's nerves on edge.

What the hell had they been doing down here?

The tunnel finally ended at a heavy steel door. Helena ran her fingers over the cold metal. It was thick and solid with an almost medieval-looking hoop handle. She couldn't sense any magical protections. Weird, but whatever.

"I'll open it and you blast anything that tries to attack us," Helena said.

Jinx raised her hands and nodded.

The door had to weigh a ton, but it swung silently open on well-oiled hinges. As a bonus, nothing came charging out to try and kill them. What did come out was an awful stench, like an open sewer next to a cat food factory.

"Ugh!" Jinx said.

That pretty well summed up Helena's feelings about the stink as well. In fact, the smell had so overloaded her senses that it took a few moments for her to notice the soft moaning and groaning.

Helena flashed the light inside and grimaced. Fifteen people were chained to the wall, covered in filth, and looking more dead than alive.

"These people are human traffickers, right?" Jinx asked. "Why would you treat your merchandise so poorly?"

Helena shook her head. "Why do people do half the awful stuff they do? Damned if I know. Run back and get Rostolov and his people. This is more than we can handle. I'll see what I can do about the anti-magic barrier."

"Okay." Jinx turned and jogged back the way they'd come.

Helena hadn't been certain what to expect from Jinx, but so far she'd been a great partner. It seemed her worries had been overblown.

Now, let's see. Taking shallow breaths, Helena entered the holding area. The people were shackled around the perimeter which likely meant she'd find the source of the magic in the center. She picked her way carefully closer, trying hard not to look at whatever was covering the floor. Ten paces in, an ethereal glow appeared in the form of a floating circle of runes.

Bingo, the spell's core. Forming a blade of ether, she slashed it through the circle. The spell burst in a harmless shower of golden sparkles. With that taken care of, Helena debated what to do next. She was decent at magical healing, but helping this many people was beyond her ability.

Before she could decide, footsteps came pounding down the tunnel. Helena quickly retreated to make room for the approaching paramedics. Best to let them do their job.

She passed a stretcher on her way to the entrance. At the trapdoor she leapt, magic carrying her out and into the fresh air. Fresher anyway. She was still in a warehouse on the docks, so the term was relative. They'd set up a winch at the edge of the opening to lift the victims to safety.

Jinx came over and said, "We didn't find any clues. What now?"

"Hopefully either one of the victims will be able to tell us something or one of the criminals will. I have no desire to take a boat out hunting for a giant octopus."

"I second that," Jinx said.

CHAPTER TEN

The fire temple looked hazy and indistinct and for some reason Daisuke was floating. He'd had enough astral interactions over the years to recognize a dream, or psychic projection if you wanted to get technical. It seemed the spirits had more on their minds. Daisuke would've preferred to never speak with them again, but he also didn't feel like expending the energy it would take to break out of the dream.

A pillar of flame appeared, towering over Daisuke, its searing heat making his astral form sweat. From within the inferno, the fire king's voice said, "Your anger holds you back, boy. Let it go and you will find spirit magic far easier."

Daisuke clenched his fists, his scarred forearms aching as he remembered the pain of his failed blessing. "You let me burn. I was just a kid! Even if I wasn't a Kugo and so worthy of your blessing, couldn't you have at least protected me from the flames?"

The fire swirled. "It's... complicated. The spirits who oversee the ceremony are bound by the ancient contract.

They can only bestow the blessing upon one of the Kugo bloodline. They lack the autonomy to do anything else, even spare an innocent from harm."

Daisuke opened his mouth to argue further, but the dreamscape started shaking like a dream earthquake was hitting the place. A moment later his eyes popped open and he found Ruq's scaly demon face inches from his. Not a sight you wanted to wake up to.

"Finally," Ruq said. "The shrine's under attack."

As if to put an exclamation point on Ruq's announcement, a flash of lightning split the darkness, followed by the familiar explosion of a fireball. Smoke billowed in the distance as something burned.

How the hell did someone find this place? Daisuke shook his head. It didn't matter now.

He stood and tried to get a sense of the battle. Four new human life forces had arrived. That wasn't too bad, assuming they weren't members of the Blood of Solomon. Four of *them* would be a problem.

First things first. He focused on Natsumi and as expected sensed her near Rio. His defensive spells settled into place and he ran toward the pair. None of the invaders were close.

"You two hurt?" Daisuke asked when he reached them.

"We're fine," Natsumi said. "What's going on?"

"Exactly what it sounds like. Four wizards have forced their way into the shrine. Best I can tell they're busy with some elemental guardians at the moment. How long the defenders will last, I'm less certain about. Stay with your dad. I'll deal with them."

Rio's condition and inability to move saved him an argument. Instead she nodded and activated defensive spells of her own. He'd do his best to make sure she didn't have to use them.

Leaving father and daughter behind, Daisuke moved swiftly and silently toward the nearest life force. Ahead of him, flashes of magic lit up the gloom and the ground trembled. He leapt over a stream and entered a small clearing where a ten-foot-tall earth elemental was trying to come to grips with a black-robed wizard.

For his part, the wizard was fleeing backwards while hurling crackling orbs of energy at the elemental only to have them burst uselessly against its rocky hide. Kind of pitiful. Why would such a weakling try attacking a place like this? There was nothing of value, at least not that Daisuke had seen.

Their reasons didn't overly concern him. Daisuke raised a hand and focused. Black lightning arced out, hammering into the wizard and burning away his life force. He crumpled to the ground, dead before he hit the dirt.

One down, three to go. Ruq was flying, invisible, above the battle. *I see someone headed for the fire temple and another two for the air temple.*

Daisuke grimaced. The temples were at opposite ends of the cavern. Terrific.

He hadn't seen Miles since the battle began, but he assumed his so-called father was around here somewhere. He'd have to take care of himself.

Daisuke ran toward the air temple. He soon spotted two figures in dark robes trying to push their way through a barrier of roaring wind. Their hands were outstretched as they chanted and tried to force a wedge of ether through the barrier.

They were making damn little progress, but the protective magic was slowly weakening. With their full focus on the temple, taking them out should be easy.

Daisuke thrust his arm forward, sending a crackling bolt of black lightning arcing toward the wizards.

The first one died instantly, but the second reacted in the nick of time, spinning a desperate shield that turned away some of the blast.

But not enough. A strangled, feminine scream tore from her throat as she flew backwards, slammed against the ground, and went limp.

He sensed a bit of life force in her. Daisuke stalked forward, ready to finish the job.

Someone killed the last one.

Had to be Miles. Given what he'd seen of the elemental guardians, he doubted the fire spirit would've been enough to handle the job so quickly. Well, he wasn't about to complain.

Now for the survivor. He moved closer and looked down at her. The blast had knocked her hood back, giving him a look at a familiar face. Her name escaped him, but he was sure she was the same girl he met during his time with the Spirit Eaters. Though he had no interest in their pointless quest to find and consume spirits, corrupting and gaining their powers in the process, they did teach him the secrets of Crimson Haze, his favorite anti-spirit spell.

The woman's eyes fluttered open then went wide when they settled on Daisuke before finally going dark as the residue of his spell consumed the last of her life force. Looked like she recognized him before she died.

He swallowed a sigh and closed her eyes. They'd been temporary allies at best and if Daisuke was being honest, he'd thought of them as little more than tools in his quest for power. Still, he felt kind of bad about killing them.

What he couldn't figure out was how the hell they found this place. Considering the magic protecting the shrine, he couldn't imagine any of these weaklings piercing the ward. He and Natsumi had only done so with the help of his tracking spell. Despite Daisuke shattering the stone wall, the ward itself remained strong.

In any case, it was none of his concern and if Natsumi hadn't been here, he'd have been happy to let them do whatever they wanted.

Footsteps crunched on the rocky ground behind him. Daisuke whirled, black lightning flashing around his hand, but it was only Miles approaching from the direction of the fire temple.

"I'm impressed. You handled three of them without a problem." Miles did his best impression of a proud father.

"How did they find this place?"

"Best guess? When you passed through the barrier some of the elemental energy must've leaked out. If they were searching for the shrine, it would've been enough to let them pinpoint its location."

"Why would they be searching for it in the first place? The group is based out of Europe. There are plenty of elemental spirits for them to hunt down closer to home."

"You know them?" Miles asked.

"Sure, I studied anti-spirit magic with the group for about six months. When I'd learned all they could teach me, I split." He shrugged. "It wasn't like we were best friends. I helped them crack a couple elemental seals they couldn't handle and they taught me the magic they'd developed. It was a good deal for both of us."

"They're evil. I'm surprised you'd have anything to do with such a group."

Daisuke laughed. "Evil? They hunt and consume spirits, not humans. I admit they're not the sweetest people I've ever dealt with, but I've seen way worse. Besides, I don't want to hear any moral judgements from a man who abandoned a couple hundred of his own children to be raised by their mothers."

Miles had the good grace to wince. "Are there more in the group?"

"They had twelve members when I was with them. Now, I couldn't say."

"You act like it's not your problem." Miles started back toward the center of the cavern where Natsumi and Rio were waiting.

"It's not. My business here is finished. Let the four clans defend this place. I plan to be on my way as soon as reinforcements arrive. If you want to hang around, that's your decision."

"What about the spirits?" Miles asked.

"What about them?"

"Nothing good can come from humans trying to seize their power for themselves."

"I can't imagine them getting it to work the way they want. The basic idea was, if a human wizard absorbed enough elemental energy, he or she would be able to control and shape physical reality with a thought. It sounded stupid to me when I first heard the idea and nothing's changed."

"What if you're wrong?" Miles asked.

"Then I'll deal with them when they become a problem."

They found Natsumi and her father unharmed. Not a surprise since none of the attackers ever got close to them.

"What was that all about?" she asked as soon as they arrived. "Who were those people and why did they attack the shrine?"

Daisuke gave her a brief rundown of the Spirit Eaters and their plans. "I don't know if the rest of the group's in Japan, but you'd best call Yoshikazu and get some guards for this place. I'll hang around until the clan arrives. After that you're on your own."

"You're just going to leave?" Natsumi asked

He nodded. "I think I've been more than helpful considering I was manipulated into coming in the first place. I'm glad you found your dad. That's what you asked me to help you do. Protecting a shrine dedicated to spirits I don't care about wasn't part of the job. I recommend calling Yoshikazu ASAP."

"The spirits have been kind enough to let me use the shrine as a base," Miles said. "I owe them. I'll stay until the threat is dealt with."

Daisuke didn't get a "loyal defender of the spirits" vibe from Miles. In fact, if you'd asked, he would've said Miles wasn't especially loyal to anything other than his quest to kill Solomon. Just went to show you couldn't always trust your first impression.

Natsumi checked her phone. "They should be awake by now. I'm going to call home. Hopefully Uncle Yoshikazu won't be too angry."

"It won't matter how angry he is," Rio said. "Given what's at stake, he'll have a team here within hours."

Natsumi grabbed Daisuke's sleeve. "Let's go outside."

He let her drag him along toward the exit. When they arrived, they found the rune gone. That would be the Spirit Eaters' doing. They obliterated the elemental seal powering the concealing magic. Repairing it wouldn't be a speedy process and until it was done, anyone could find this place.

Out on the trail Natsumi finally let go. "You're really going to leave?"

"Yeah, I am. Was I unclear about that earlier?" He sighed at her disappointed frown. "Look, these guys aren't that tough. Even if they come back after I leave, a Kugo security team should be enough to deal with them. I assume the other clans will send help as well. My presence is not at all required. Remember, this was supposed to be a quick visit, find your dad, then I leave with no one the wiser."

"The situation's changed."

Daisuke shook his head. "Not that much. If the Spirit Eaters are here now, then they knew about the shrine before we arrived. They've probably been aware of it since Miles moved in. The same things would've happened even if I wasn't here."

"But you are here."

"Not for long. Make your call and keep my name out of it. I'd prefer to avoid an international incident."

She shook her head. "Fine, have it your way."

Natsumi walked a little ways off to call home. Daisuke should follow her example and call the boss, but he wasn't ready for that conversation yet.

CHAPTER ELEVEN

Helena stood beside the trapdoor and did her best to ignore the acrid stench of filth and despair rising from the tunnel below. Rescue workers used a winch to lift semiconscious victims out one at a time. She'd seen undead that looked healthier than these unfortunate people.

Jinx wrinkled her nose in disgust. "Why do they have to keep them in such miserable conditions?"

Helena's jaw clenched as she surveyed the depressing stream of humanity. "I don't know, but I can't believe it was random. Someone went to a lot of trouble to torture these people. Criminals, evil as they are, want money and power. This brings neither, at least as far as I can see."

As one of the last victims was carried out, a glimmer in the ether caught Helena's eye. A strange mark on the woman's hand glowed in her magical vision. She didn't recognize the design at a glance, but it was the first interesting thing she'd seen.

"Sergeant Rostolov," she said. "I'd like to take a closer look at the woman they just brought up."

He nodded and barked an order. The paramedic wheeled her off to the side and Helena strode over with Jinx.

She leaned in, studying the mark. It kind of looked like a demon seal, but she hadn't studied the Book of Wisdom like the boss and couldn't remember what they all looked like.

Jinx hovered at her shoulder, a deep frown creasing her beautiful face. "The magic feels the same as the octopus. I bet it was looking for this woman."

"You might be right," Helena said. "But the more pressing question is why? What's so special about her that she'd be marked by Dagon's cult and how did she end up in the hands of human traffickers?"

"When you say it like that, it seems like we haven't learned anything valuable."

"I don't mean to be negative," Helena said. "But there is a lot of work left to be done."

She glanced at Rostolov and waved him over. "Ma'am?"

"This woman has been marked by the cult of Dagon. She may well be what the octopus is looking for. Moving her away from the water as quickly as possible and keeping her secure is vital. Once she recovers, I'll need to speak with her."

"What's special about her?" Rostolov asked.

"I have no idea." Helena took her phone out and snapped several pictures of the mark along with a few shots of the woman's face. With any luck the boss would be able to figure out what the mark meant and who she was. She attached the images to a brief text updating her on their status and sent it off.

Jinx kept darting looks toward the water. Helena had a pretty good idea what was on her mind. The demonic octopus could return at any moment. That it hadn't yet was a minor miracle, one that couldn't hold. Hopefully once the woman was gone, it would ensure the creature stayed away.

Helena pocketed her phone. "Let's take a look outside. I doubt there's anything useful, but no stone unturned and all that."

They picked their way across the devastated dock, skirting jagged holes and twisted metal. The stench of brine and scorched flesh hung heavy in the air. The smell wasn't as bad as the underground chamber, but it wasn't pleasant either.

Helena extended her senses, probing the ether for any lingering traces of the octopus's corruption. There wasn't much and the little she found quickly petered out about a hundred yards into the sea.

"I really don't want to go fishing for that thing, but I was hoping we might be able to figure out where it came from," Helena said.

"Corruption fades quickly once the source is gone," Jinx said. "It's both a blessing and a curse that it doesn't linger."

"True. I'm not sure what to do next and the uncertainty is getting on my nerves."

Helena turned back to the warehouse and found Sergeant Rostolov headed their way.

"What's up?" Helena asked.

"One of the smugglers came to. He's still pretty out of it, but I figured you'd want to know."

"Thank you, Sergeant. Maybe he'll have something useful to say."

Rostolov led them to a black prisoner transport van. It was nothing special aside from being built like a tank. He yanked open the rear doors, revealing the unconscious figures of the smugglers lying chained to a heavy steel bar running the length of the van.

One of the men was sitting up, his eyes glassy and unfocused. He looked young, maybe Helena's age but not much more. His cheap suit hadn't come through the fight undamaged and pale skin poked out here and there.

Helena climbed in for a closer look. She wasn't going to get anything useful out of him like this. A burst of healing magic repaired the absolute minimum necessary to clear his thoughts. He gave a final shake of his head and focused on her with now-clear eyes.

"Feeling better?" she asked.

He nodded. Good, he spoke English. That would make things easier.

"Let's talk about the dungeon under your warehouse. What were you doing with all those people?"

The man swallowed hard. "I don't know much. The wizard told us to keep them like that so their despair would fuel the protection spell."

Helena had never heard of a barrier spell powered by human misery. Usually when you cast such a spell you connected it directly to the ether to provide power.

"The wizard who created the barrier, was it Remi, the one who sold you the demon? You'd know him better as the Devil's Shadow."

The man shook his head. "No, the protection spell was older. The demon was supposed to deal with the monsters attacking our boats. It wasn't the octopus, that thing's new."

"Tell me about the other monsters," Helena said.

"Ugly things. Imagine an eel and a person had a baby and you've got an idea what they looked like." He shuddered. "Bullets bounced off them, but you could knock them back into the water and outrun them. At least that's all we could figure out how to do. We bought the barrier because they kept crawling onto the docks and killing our lookouts. Don't ask me what we did to piss them off. I have no idea. The boss might be able to tell you more."

Helena's mind raced as she tried to make sense of everything they'd learned so far. She backed out of the van and Rostolov closed the door again.

"Have you heard anything about other boats being attacked or going missing?" Helena asked.

Rostolov shook his head. "No, but the coast guard might've. That's not my beat. I only deal with stuff onshore. I can ask if you'd like."

"Please do, thank you," Helena said.

She ran a hand through her hair and swallowed a sigh. Now it was a waiting game. Until someone woke up or she heard from the boss, there was nothing else Helena could do.

The chime of Angelique's phone distracted her from the report she'd been reading. It wasn't all that interesting, just Donny's findings on the enchanted compass Daisuke brought back from the Temple of Abaddon. Apparently it could be used to track down anyone with the blood of Solomon. It was currently locked on Daisuke and Donny had yet to determine how to change it to someone else.

Setting the paper aside, she picked up her phone. The text was from Helena and there were images attached. She swiped through them.

The first was of a symbol that looked vaguely like a demon seal. Angelique grabbed the Book of Wisdom from its spot on the corner of her desk and turned to the index in the back. There was a handy chart with all the symbols lined up along with the page number if you wanted to look up more details. It was a remarkably convenient setup for a book of magic. Most wizards seemed to want to make their writing as difficult for you to understand as possible.

It took no time at all to confirm that the symbol wasn't for one of the seventy-two demons. That was a problem since it meant she had no idea what the symbol actually meant. Assuming they were right about Dagon's involvement, and everything indicated they were, it had to be something to do with his cult. The Circle hadn't fought with Dagon's followers to amount to anything since she founded the group. There were so many problems to deal with on land, they didn't bother much with the water.

She closed the book and transferred the woman's picture to her laptop. From there she emailed it to Crystal along with a request to use the facial recognition software to identify her.

Unfortunately that was all she could do from her end. A short text to Helena confirmed the mark wasn't one of the seventy-two and promised to contact her when she had more information on the woman.

Angelique sighed. Sometimes it was so frustrating not being able to help her agents as much as she'd like to. But she couldn't conjure information out of thin air. She was about to set her phone down when it rang. It was Daisuke's ringtone.

A twenty-four-hour check-in. That was pretty good for him, though she'd been expecting a text.

"Daisuke, how goes the search?"

"It's over, Boss. We found Rio late yesterday and you'll

never believe who was with him. My father." Angelique's heart skipped a beat. "I sensed no lie when he spoke and he at least superficially matches the man Mom described. I confirmed it with a resonance spell. At a minimum, we're closely related."

"Okay, Daisuke, slow down. I'm going to need you to tell me everything. Start at the beginning and leave nothing out." How did his voice sound so calm? It wasn't every day you met your long-lost father.

Daisuke ran through it all for her, ending with the attack on the elemental shrine. "So that's how my day went. It was a little more eventful than I expected, but all in all not terrible."

Angelique stared at the phone then rubbed her eyes. In all her eternal existence she'd never met anyone who attracted trouble like this boy. She wasn't sure if he was cursed, blessed, or something in between.

"Boss? You there?"

"Yes. I needed a moment to wrap my head around everything you said. To be clear, you met your father, found out Solomon the Great is your uncle, located Rio who was in the process of having his missing arm regrown—a spell that, had you asked me, I would've sworn didn't exist—you then made an arrangement with your father to eventually hunt down your uncle, and finally the shrine was attacked by four members of the Spirit Eaters who you killed. Did I miss anything?"

"I only killed three of them, but otherwise bang on, Boss. Natsumi called in Kugo reinforcements. I'll be back as soon as they show up, figure six or so hours."

"No, Daisuke, I need you to hunt down the other Spirit Eaters and deal with them."

There was a long moment of silence before he asked,

"Why? They're wimps. Should they be dumb enough to attack the shrine again, Kugo security forces will be able to deal with them no problem."

"Some things have changed since you left the group. For one thing, they have a new leader. His name is Ahmed Antar and he's Egyptian. The group left Europe a year ago for Egypt at his command. Six months ago, we're pretty sure they stole an artifact from a private collector. Anatoly has been observing the group, trying to figure out if they had it and if so where. His last report was from two weeks ago when the group vanished. That's about when Rio went missing, right?"

"Yup. What's this artifact supposed to do?" Angelique could tell from his tone that Daisuke was in serious mode now. Good, he needed to be.

"Our research indicates that it's an elemental battery of sorts. Basically it can absorb, store, and release a huge amount of spirit energy. From the sounds of it, the shrine is directly connected to the elemental realms. Assuming they gain access, they could be able to draw out a virtually unlimited supply of power."

"Well, shit. If there's one thing those idiots shouldn't have access to, it's unlimited power. Looks like my early return trip is on hold. Is it cool if I share the details with the clan? Worst comes to worst they'll need to know what they're up against."

"By all means. None of this is a secret. Don't underestimate them, Daisuke. Whatever they might have been when you were with them, Ahmed has turned them into something truly dangerous. They murdered at least ten people in the process of stealing the artifact."

"Charming. Before I go, what's this thing look like?"

"It's an orb made of clear crystal. It changes color based on the element it's storing. Our research indicates it can only hold one kind at a time."

"That's something. How are the girls doing?"

"They haven't run into anything they can't handle yet." In her sternest tone Angelique added, "Don't worry about them. You need to look after your own situation."

"Sure, Boss, no problem. I'll be in touch. Later."

The line went dead and she set the phone on her desk and rubbed her eyes again. Why did everything have to happen at the same time?

CHAPTER TWELVE

Daisuke stood on the trail a few yards past the elemental shrine's entrance. He'd just finished his report to the boss. To his considerable surprise, she informed him that he was staying in Japan to deal with the Spirit Eaters rather than telling him to come straight back. How in the world the group ended up a big enough threat to attract the Circle's attention was something he'd never understand. When Daisuke was a member, all they had was ambition and a little talent for anti-spirit magic. He also didn't know why she hadn't mentioned his former associates were under observation, but the boss didn't answer to him.

He looked out over the park. The rising sun painted the sky in soft hues of pink and orange while birds chirped away like he wasn't going to have to hunt down and kill a bunch of people he used to think of as allies. It was a funny old world, no doubt about it.

"Don't pretend you're not a little relieved to get the order," Ruq said. "You didn't want to leave the job half done."

"What I wanted was to go home in case Helena and Jinx

need backup. While I admit what you said is true, it's not my priority. Or it wasn't anyway."

"Think she'll let you keep the artifact?" Ruq asked.

Daisuke grinned. "Not a chance. Pity, but I'm sure it's going straight into the vault."

Ruq landed on his shoulder in rat form before he turned and strode back into the shrine. At the end of the tunnel, Natsumi and Miles were standing near the spell circle healing Rio. They all looked his way as he entered. Natsumi's eyes flashed with annoyance and she crossed her arms.

"We have a problem," Daisuke said. "According to the boss, the Spirit Eaters have stolen an artifact capable of absorbing elemental energy, like a lot of it. If they reach the shrine, Japan might be in trouble."

Natsumi arched an eyebrow. "Let me guess, she ordered you to stay and deal with them. And, unlike when I asked for your help stopping them, you're going to do it."

Daisuke shrugged. "That's right. I work for the Circle, not you. When do the guards arrive?"

"Uncle Yoshikazu said a few hours. He's calling the other clan heads, but their compounds are further away, so we'll be on our own for a day or so."

"That's not ideal, but it is what it is. I assume he's going to arrange to lock down the park."

"Obviously," Natsumi said, still sounding annoyed. "We can't have a battle with civilians running around everywhere."

"Good." Daisuke stayed calm, refusing to give her the satisfaction of pissing him off. "I'll make my preparations while we're waiting."

"Perhaps I can help." Miles motioned for Daisuke to follow him deeper into the shrine.

Daisuke didn't need any help, but he figured Miles had something he wanted to ask about away from the others. They left together, Natsumi's angry glare burning a hole in Daisuke's back.

When they were out of earshot Miles asked, "Did you tell Angelique about me?"

Daisuke directed their path back toward where he left the woman's body. "Of course I did. I can't keep secrets from her and do what I do. Well, not about important things anyway."

"And?"

"And what?"

"What did she have to say about our arrangement?"

"If you can help us find Solomon the Great, she was all for it. Speaking of, how long are you hanging around here?"

"Until Rio is fully recovered. The ethereal flow must be precisely managed or his arm won't regrow properly. It's only for a few more days and I did promise to see him set to rights."

Miles's determination to honor his promise to Rio made Daisuke more confident he'd follow through with their arrangement. It was possible he'd come to regret his choice to trust the man, but for now he was content to go with his gut.

They reached the woman's body. It hadn't moved, thank goodness. He'd had this vague sense that he'd arrive and find it gone, sunk into the ground and consumed by earth spirits.

Daisuke drew his dagger and conjured flames to purify it and burn Natsumi's blood off. That done, he poked the corpse to collect a fresh sample.

"What good will that do?" Miles asked.

"Her brother is a member of the group as well. Or at least he was when I was with them. If he still is, I can use a tracking spell to find him, assuming he wasn't one of the guys I already killed. I didn't check them very closely."

"You talk about killing very nonchalantly," Miles said. "Does taking a life not bother you?"

"It used to," Daisuke said. "But it turns out killing is like anything else. If you do it enough times, it becomes routine. Like, this evil asshole needs to die, so I kill him. Similar to a rabid dog, putting him down is a community service."

"That's cold-blooded, son."

Daisuke smiled. Was he going to try playing the worried father now? Miles was about ten years too late for it to make any difference. "Life doesn't allow for weakness, not in this line of work. The only good enemies are dead ones and even then, sometimes the bastards come back to life. If you're soft, it's asking for trouble."

A bit of ethereal manipulation activated a new tracking spell. Happily, the knife didn't point toward any of the already dead people. He got the sense that the enemy waited somewhere about fifteen to twenty miles away. Not that far, but not close enough to allow an easy strike either.

Prep work done, Daisuke strode back toward the exit. Natsumi was beside her father who had sat back down on the grass. "What was that about?" she asked.

"I needed to figure out where the rest of them were hiding." Daisuke held up the bloody dagger and told her his best guess on how far away they were. "Shouldn't take long to home in on them. The only thing I'm worried about is whether they've added any new members. If it's just the Egyptian and the eight I knew, taking them down won't be a huge problem."

"Why would they send such a small force here?" Natsumi asked.

"Scouting party," Daisuke said. "I'm sure they were uncertain what sort of defenses they'd find. If it was too dangerous, they could fall back and attack together. Of course, with Miles and me here, they didn't have that chance, but they couldn't have known ahead of time. Either that or Ahmed didn't like those four and wanted them out of the way. Personally, I think it's the former."

"When you go, I'm coming with you," Natsumi said.

Daisuke shook his head. "Don't take this the wrong way, but you'd just be something else I need to worry about. Remember our little duel? These people are the ones who taught me the spell I used on your fire cat. Spirit magic is the worst possible option for fighting them. Stay here and help protect the shrine. Even the Spirit Eaters aren't enough to handle an entire Kugo security team."

Natsumi was scowling at him but at least she wasn't arguing. He'd take that as a win.

CHAPTER THIRTEEN

Muted sunlight filtered through the dingy curtains of the cheap Odessa hotel room as Helena ran a brush through her tangled hair. She'd managed a few hours' sleep last night, but it had been far from the best night of her life. You'd think the police would've at least sprung for a nicer hotel given how eager they were for her and Jinx's help.

Her cellphone rang, seeming far louder than usual this morning. She tossed the brush down and grabbed her phone. Rostolov's name was on the screen.

"Sergeant?" Helena asked.

"The trafficker chief is awake and ready for questioning."

"Excellent. Could you send a car around for us?"

"Not a problem. Someone will be there in fifteen minutes or so."

"Thanks. Any word on the victims?" she asked.

"Nothing from the hospital as of this morning, but the rest of the traffickers are awake as well should you wish to speak to more than the bossman."

"I doubt they'd have more information than he does but thank you. See you later." She disconnected and sighed. Getting a handle on the truth of the situation was proving trickier than she'd expected.

Giving up on her hair, Helena stuffed her phone into her jacket pocket and grabbed her room key. A few strides down the hallway brought her to Jinx's room. She knocked and it swung open to reveal Jinx, dressed, prepped, and wearing a new outfit. Dark pants and a red top today.

Helena arched an eyebrow. "Where'd you get the new clothes?"

"I shadow walked home for a quick change while you were sleeping. I would've picked you up something but I've never visited your apartment so shadow walking there is a problem."

Helena tamped down a flare of annoyance. She'd never thought much about the sheer convenience of being able to run home in the blink of an eye. She'd always thought of shadow walking as a way to reach the job quickly, but it seemed it had more mundane uses as well.

"Rostolov is sending a car for us. The head trafficker finally woke up." Helena turned toward the lobby and Jinx fell in beside her. "Did you sleep well last night?"

"Last night wasn't a sleep night for me. I'm good for another three days."

Right, half-demon. Jinx looked so human it was easy to forget she wasn't.

The hotel's lobby was every bit as forgettable as the rest of it. Helena strode right through without so much as a glance around. Outside, she took a breath of polluted air and sighed. Zurich wasn't that much bigger than Odessa, but it was so much nicer. Of course, that meant the Circle seldom had anything to do locally. Which was fine with Helena. No one wanted chaos where they lived.

An unmarked police car pulled up beside the hotel and Helena opened the passenger-side door. Jinx climbed in the back and they were on their way. The driver never said a word as he wove through the morning traffic. Helena assumed that was because he didn't speak English.

Soon enough the tires screeched against the pavement as the car pulled up to the curb outside a blocky greenish gray precinct building. It had all the charm of a cinder block painted vomit green. They exited the vehicle and strode toward the front door. Beside the check-in area, Rostolov waited to greet them.

"Good morning," Helena said. "I didn't expect the prisoners to recover this quickly."

Rostolov grunted. "I'm not sure recovered is the right word. One of his hands has turned black and looks in danger of falling off. But he is awake and conscious."

"I can work with that," Helena said. "Lead the way."

Rostolov led them through a side door and down a bare hallway. Their footsteps sounded hollow on the cold linoleum.

"I made some inquiries yesterday. No ships have been reported missing in the past six months. It seems the smugglers' enemy has no interest in harming anyone else."

"If we're right and it's the cult of Dagon, you can be sure they have an interest in harming whoever they can. The fact that they haven't done so is strange." Helena shook her head. "Trying to figure out the thinking of a demon cult will only give you a headache."

They reached the interrogation room, a square room lit only by a bare lightbulb dangling from the ceiling. It fit perfectly with the building's overall look. A single man sat chained to a very sturdy steel table positioned directly under the lightbulb.

The traffickers' boss had seen better days. His suit had been exchanged for an orange prison coverall. He looked up as they approached, his dark, bloodshot eyes somewhat unfocused. His twisted, blackened hand rested on the table beside him. As best she could tell it wasn't causing him any pain.

Helena sat in the chair opposite him, her gaze locking with his. "We have questions," she said. "If you're helpful, I'll remove that hand before the corruption reaches your heart and kills you."

The man's Adam's apple bobbed as he swallowed. His gaze flicked to Jinx, an understandable action from any man with a pulse, before returning to Helena. "Ask what you will. I've already lost everything for him, I have no interest in losing my life as well."

Helena frowned. She'd thought he was the top man, but from the sounds of it, she'd been mistaken. "Let's start with the obvious questions. What's your name and who is the "him" you mentioned?"

"My name is Petruk. The Russian, Ivankov, is my employer. He controls most of the crime in Ukraine as well as the border towns."

Helena shot a look at Rostolov who shook his head.

Interesting as the details of Eastern European crime were, dealing with nonmagical criminals wasn't Helena's job. "Who created the barrier around your warehouse?"

"A wizard named Sava Rude. Mr. Ivankov introduced us. I got the impression he handled magical things for the organization." Petruk grimaced. "He was… a creepy fellow, but the barrier did keep those creatures from killing our look-outs so at least he knew his business. He said we had to surround the spell circle with suffering prisoners to keep it working. I didn't get the impression questions would be welcome, so we just did as we were told. And it worked."

Helena's jaw clenched, but she immediately forced herself to relax. She'd seen enough casual evil that their complete disregard for human life shouldn't shock her.

"Why those specific prisoners?" Jinx asked.

Petruk shrugged, his chains rattling as he did. "There was nothing special about them. We selected the ones we thought would bring the lowest profit at the auction. Ugly women, cripples, that sort of thing."

"Where did they come from?" Helena asked.

"We raid fishing villages and border towns. No one cares what happens to those people and they won't be missed in any case."

Fishing villages? Hmm. Helena tapped her chin. Isolated fishing villages were the kind of places Dagon's worship might catch on. If so, kidnapping his followers was exactly the sort of thing the Lord of Corrupt Oceans would take badly.

"Where are these fishing villages?" Helena asked.

"On islands out in the Black Sea. We spot them by heli-copter then send the raiders in. Easy money."

"Okay," Helena said. "Tell me more about Sava Rude and your Russian master. Starting with where I can find them."

"I have no idea where you can find Mr. Ivankov. All I have is a number where I reach his assistant. If he wants to talk to me, he calls me back. As for Sava, he works out of a village about twenty miles beyond the border called Staryol. Creepy place. I didn't see a single soul when we visited. Felt like a ghost town."

Helena considered for a moment then turned to Jinx. "I can't think of anything else at the moment, can you?"

Jinx shook her head. "No, I'm good."

"A promise is a promise." Helena stood and stepped around the table. "Besides, I don't want you dying on the off chance I think of more questions. Now hold still."

Helena closed her eyes and focused. Before anyone could react, a golden blade sliced Petruk's hand off at the wrist, an inch above the edge of the blackened flesh. Next she seared the end to prevent any bleeding. Finally she checked the rest of his body for any lingering corruption. She didn't find much, but made sure to neutralize it just to be safe.

When she finished, Petruk was gasping in pain. But he was also out of danger. Helena could've blocked the pain but saw no reason to. Let him enjoy a taste of what he gave his victims.

"We're done here. Sergeant Rostolov, I'd appreciate it if you could look up Sava Rude and Ivankov. Any information you can provide would be helpful. The location of Staryol would be good as well."

Rostolov's usually dour face was extra grim. "I'll do the best I can, but most of this is happening outside the city and the country. I doubt our records will have anything useful. As for Ivankov, that's a fairly common name. Without more to go on, I'm not sure where to start."

"Anything you can find out would be welcome. We'll do some digging on our end as well. I'd like to check on the woman from yesterday, the one with Dagon's mark."

"The driver can take you whenever you're ready,"

Rostolov said. "He's been assigned to you for the duration of your stay."

"Does he speak English? He didn't say a word the whole way over here."

"Of course he does. Assigning someone who only spoke Ukrainian wouldn't be very helpful. Borys's best quality is his disinterest in casual chatter."

Helena smiled. "That's a relief. Let's meet up for lunch and compare notes."

"Tell Borys to take you to the Metro Cafe. I'll be there at noon."

"Got it. And good luck," Helena said.

"To us both," Rostolov said.

CHAPTER FOURTEEN

Angelique's phone chimed when a new text hit. She'd been rereading Anatoly's report on the Spirit Eaters. The details were depressingly thin, especially regarding their new leader. Nothing beyond hearsay and guesses. She doubted there was enough to bother sending it to Daisuke.

Setting the folder down on her desk, she grabbed her phone and read a text from Helena. She was looking for background on a criminal named Ivankov, a wizard for hire called Sava Rude, and a town named Staryol. None of the names rang a bell for her. Hardly surprising given the number of criminals and wizards in the world.

How did an investigation into the cult of Dagon expand so much? A wizard selling his services to criminals was always concerning, but it was usually a job for the locals to handle. Still, she trusted Helena to keep her eye on the goal. Sometimes you had to follow a lot of threads to find the one that led to the prize.

Angelique left her office and made her way to the basement steps. She could hear faint murmurs from the store. Sounded like they had some business today. Arcane Books and Trinkets made a good cover for the Circle, but it was also nice when it turned a profit.

It was a short walk down to Crystal's computer lab. She knocked then pushed the door open. Readouts glowed and server racks hummed as their resident computer genius worked in front of a huge monitor. When she didn't have a specific task, Crystal searched the web for any information about dangerous magical artifacts, in particular any involving Solomon's demons.

"Crystal." She jumped and spun her chair around.

"You startled me, Boss." Crystal peered at her through thick glasses. "Everything okay?"

"Unfortunately, no. I need you to run a search on a criminal named Ivankov in the area of Ukraine."

Crystal hid the program she'd been working in and opened a new browser window. Angelique knew little about computers, but Crystal assured her the custom browser was far more secure than any off-the-shelf solution.

A few keystrokes and the machine did its thing. "Not seeing anything specific beyond a fellow who was arrested for drunk driving five years ago. Nothing about the story screams criminal mastermind."

"How about a wizard named Sava Rude?"

Another search and a shake of the head. "The name doesn't even show up."

Angelique swallowed a sigh. This was going about as well as she expected. "Okay, last but not least a town called Staryol."

Crystal typed then clicked, her eyes scanning the monitor. "Here it is. Looks like Staryol is a small town, population under five hundred. Remote, just over the Russian border. Pretty close to the radiation zone, but still safe for humans."

Angelique was about to apologize for wasting Crystal's time when she said, "This is interesting. Apparently not long after World War Three, an NGO tied to the UN tried to relocate the survivors, but get this, the people of Staryol refused to leave. Claimed the village was on holy ground."

"Holy ground?" There was no such thing as holy ground —as a former angel she should know—though it was possible to charge a barrier with holy magic. That might trick credulous mortals into believing something miraculous was happening. At a minimum it didn't sound like the sort of place an evil wizard would set up shop. "I'm not aware of anything like that in the area."

"Apparently the people in charge didn't want to force the issue and they were left alone. Been there ever since."

"Pull up a satellite image of Staryol." Angelique moved closer to peer over Crystal's shoulder.

A few keystrokes later, a bird's-eye view of a small village filled the screen. It was little more than a cluster of rough-hewn houses arranged in a haphazard circle. No signs of life, but the well-worn paths between buildings suggested the town hadn't been fully abandoned, though if even close to five hundred people called the place home she'd be shocked.

"Pull back."

Crystal tapped a key and the view expanded. No farms or anything resembling industry in the area. How did the people survive? Something about Staryol gave her a bad feeling.

"Okay, what about the Black Sea islands? Anything interesting?"

Crystal shook her head. "There are hundreds of them,

and most have at least a small village. I need more to go on to pick out which, if any, might be worshipping Dagon."

Angelique sighed. So many questions and damn few answers.

"Thanks, Crystal."

"Glad to help. I feel like I've been less than useful lately."

Angelique gave her shoulder a squeeze then retreated to her office to call Helena.

"Boss?" Helena asked.

"Crystal did some digging but we didn't find much. She identified hundreds of islands in the Black Sea and we have no idea which you need to investigate. Ivankov and Sava are mysteries. Staryol has an interesting backstory, but I saw nothing that excited me about the place and I can't imagine why a wizard of any talent would make it his base beyond the remoteness of the village."

"Thanks, Boss. I didn't have super high hopes but figured it couldn't hurt to ask. We're on our way to try and speak with the woman marked by Dagon's cult. Hopefully she'll be awake and in a chatty mood."

"Good luck and keep me informed."

"Will do, Boss."

The line went dead and Angelique set her phone on the table. Helena was an experienced field agent and she had Jinx backing her up. They should be okay.

At least, Angelique dearly hoped they would be.

Helena pocketed her phone and glanced out the window at the drab Odessa skyline. She'd been hoping for more information even as she hadn't expected to get it. Though she didn't know the full extent of the Circle's resources, Helena would've been surprised if they had much in this part of the world, not when there were so many problems elsewhere.

"What did she say?" Jinx asked.

"Not a lot." Helena gave her a rundown of their limited intel. "If the woman can't tell us more, I'm not sure what we're going to do."

"I hope she's recovered," Jinx said. "Having something like that done to you has to take a toll."

Helena had no doubt that was the truth.

Soon enough Borys pulled up beside a ten-story tower of glass and white stone. Odessa General Hospital was one of the few interesting-looking buildings she'd seen. Helena and Jinx climbed out, but before they could leave, Borys rolled down his window and said, "I will wait in the parking garage. Text me when you're ready for pickup."

"That's perfect, thanks," Helena said before turning back to march toward the entrance.

Inside the lobby, a uniformed police officer stood near the reception desk. He nodded at their approach. The two nurses on duty said nothing as they stared at Helena and Jinx.

"Sergeant Rostolov said to expect you," the officer said in thickly accented but still understandable English. "This way."

He led them toward the elevators at the rear of the lobby. Once the doors had closed he said, "She's in a private room on the fourth floor. We kept them all on the same floor for security reasons, but she's been isolated."

"Perfect," Helena said. She had no idea how involved the woman was with the cult of Dagon and had even less interest in her causing trouble for the others.

The chime sounded and the doors slid open. The sharp scent of cleaning products and antiseptic hit her as soon as they stepped into the hall. The area was silent save for the beeping of computer monitors.

At the end of the hall, the officer pushed open the victim's door. The woman was lying in her bed, eyes open but seemingly looking at nothing. She had the distant, glassy-eyed appearance of someone not fully conscious. Her dark hair was splayed across the pillow and her sunken, hollow-cheeked face was plain and bruised. Nothing about her screamed evil cultist. In truth she was more pitiful than threatening.

Helena entered with Jinx a step behind. She plastered on her best smile. "Hello there, I'm Helena and this is my partner, Jinx. We're hoping to ask a few questions, if you're feeling up to it."

The woman stared back, her dark eyes vacant and clearly not understanding a word Helena had said.

Helena muttered a spell and the ether swirled around her before settling into her mouth and ears.

The woman's eyes went wide at the sight of the ethereal sparks. She gasped and cowered back against the pillows, pulling the covers up to her eyes.

"I... I didn't know you were a priestess," the woman stammered as the magic translated her words into English. "Please, forgive me for not showing proper respect! I meant no offense!"

Tears leaked from the corners of her eyes as she shrank back in excessive terror. It seemed she expected Helena to punish her severely. That reaction made it clear she'd had some interactions with hellpriests.

Helena held up her hands in a calming gesture. "Easy

now, I'm not a priestess, I'm a wizard. And we're not here to hurt you, only to ask some questions. Okay?"

The woman lowered the covers slightly, peering at Helena with a mix of fear and confusion in her dark, frightened eyes. "You have magic, I saw it. That makes you a priestess."

"I'm not a priestess, I swear. My magic is different." A deep discussion into the nature of magic didn't seem like the best idea at the moment, so she asked, "What's your name?"

The woman hesitated, maybe thinking this was some sort of test. Finally, she whispered, "Vika."

"Vika, my friend and I are here to help you. Can you tell us what happened, how you ended up in the warehouse basement?" Helena kept her voice soft and soothing. Some of the fear had already drained out of Vika's expression.

"I don't know how long ago it happened," Vika started hesitantly. "Weeks at least. It was late evening when a strange boat showed up at our dock. It was bigger than any of the fishing boats. Strange boats never showed up at our village. Our priest and the mayor weren't sure what to do. Before they could make up their minds, men with guns came on deck. They shot anyone who resisted, even the priest. I didn't think anyone could defeat his magic, but they kept shooting and shooting until he eventually fell."

She went silent, tears leaking down her face. Helena couldn't deny her surprise to find someone crying over a dead hellpriest. Those were generally the only good ones.

Helena stayed silent as Vika got herself under control. "The invaders captured the rest of the villagers and burned everything to the ground. We were brought to the warehouse and separated into two groups. My group was dragged to the basement and chained up. They left us to die slowly with no food and only enough water to prolong the process. I had prepared myself for death, then people came and freed us. I thought it was a miracle."

"I noticed the mark on your hand. Could you tell me about it?" Helena asked.

Vika pulled her arm out from under the covers and moved it closer to Helena. "I was recently chosen to begin training as an underpriestess. Even though I have no magic it is still a great honor."

Helena had no idea what an underpriestess did, but she could feel the corruption in the mark. On the other hand, Vika struck her as the least likely servant of a demon lord she'd ever met. Little about this made sense.

"Congratulations," Helena said. "Would you mind telling me about your religion?"

For the first time since she arrived, Vika perked up, even offering an eager smile that made her plain face light up. "We worship the God of the Ocean. In exchange for sacrifices he makes sure our fishing boats come back home safely. Being chosen to serve him is a great honor."

"I'm sure it is. What sort of sacrifices do you offer?"

Vika's smile withered and Helena feared she'd stepped into some taboo subject. "I don't know, only the priests do. One of them goes out alone in the fishing boat once a month to offer the god his sacrifice. The details are a secret. Once I'd completed my training, I'm sure I would've learned the truth before I was sent to my permanent post."

Helena frowned. "I don't understand. You don't serve your home village?"

"No, we're sent to one of the neighboring villages. It's hard to guide people who have known you your whole life." Vika let out a long yawn and her eyes started to droop.

"You're looking tired. I apologize for the long discussion. One more question and I'll leave you to rest. How can I find your village?"

"I wish I could tell you, but this is the first time I've ever left home. I couldn't find my way back on my own."

Helena nodded and patted her hand. "It's okay. Thank you for your time."

She led Jinx out into the hall and the other woman said, "I followed none of that. Did you learn anything important?"

"A bit." Helena repeated what Vika had told her, as much to get it all straight in her head as to share information.

"I've never heard of anything like what you described," Jinx said. "It's not brutal enough for a demon cult. What do you think?"

"I think underpriestess is another word for sacrifice and if she hadn't gotten kidnapped, Vika would likely be at the bottom of the Black Sea right now feeding a giant octopus. We need to go back to the station and speak with our one-handed friend about the raid. He might be able to tell us where to find the island."

CHAPTER FIFTEEN

Daisuke watched from the trail above as a convoy of six shiny black sedans poured into the parking lot in front of Mount Fuji. Kugo security forces spilled out of them like white-suited ants. He counted twenty of them, double the standard team. The Kugo clan was taking no chances.

Natsumi stepped onto the trail, her face grim. "I have to tell Uncle Yoshikazu it was you who brought me here. Given everything that's happened I can't think of a way around it."

Daisuke shrugged. "I figured as much. You're the one who'll have to deal with the flack, not me. Do what you think best."

"I thought you'd be more upset." She sounded a bit disappointed.

He smiled. "Why? Keeping my presence a secret would've been ideal, but it was far from a necessity. When the authorities find the Spirit Eaters' bodies, knowing who killed them will make the investigation way easier. Anyway, the cavalry's here so it's time for me to go."

"Aren't you going to say goodbye to Miles?"

Daisuke cocked his head. "Why would I?"

"What do you mean why? He's your father."

Daisuke snorted. "Maybe technically, but he's nothing more than a stranger to me. We've made arrangements to contact each other if necessary and that's enough."

"If you say so. Will I see you again before you leave?"

"Not unless things go badly. I'll be in touch in any case."

"Be careful." He was surprised that she sounded like she meant it, despite her earlier annoyance.

"I'll do my best. Later." Daisuke cast an invisibility spell, leapt into the air, and soared away without a backward glance.

Daisuke flew westward, guided by the tug of his tracking spell. It was a lucky thing the Spirit Eaters weren't too far off. Maintaining three spells at once was a drain.

The cityscape blurred beneath him, a patchwork of gleaming skyscrapers and cramped residential blocks, interspersed with pockets of green.

The neighborhoods grew gradually worse until the spell led him to a decrepit storefront in an area marked for redevelopment. Graffiti marred the boarded-up windows and weeds sprouted from cracks in the sidewalk. To the average passerby, it was just another urban eyesore, but Daisuke's tracking spell confirmed the target was inside.

He landed in front of the place and released all three spells. He sensed the life forces of nine people inside along with a powerful magical presence. The latter had to be the artifact. Looked like they'd only added one new member. Good. Nine was plenty.

Daisuke weighed his options. A frontal assault was risky.

Nine against one, even when they were weaklings, wasn't great odds. Best to have a closer look.

"Ruq," he said. "Take a peek, but don't do anything aggressive. Demons are as vulnerable to anti-spirit magic as elementals."

"Don't worry, I'm in no hurry to return to Abaddon's hell." Ruq flew off, silent and invisible.

While he had a minute, Daisuke summoned his trunk and pulled out the Staff of Law. This was one of those occasions when even the modest power boost it provided would be worthwhile.

Found them.

A faint tingle in the back of his mind preceded his awareness merging with Ruq's. An image unfurled in his mind as Ruq shared his sight. The shop's interior had been gutted, creating a cavernous space. Fifty yards in, the Spirit Eaters were clustered together, their faces lit by the golden glow of a scrying portal.

Eight of them were obviously European, assuming their pale skin and fair hair was any indication. The ninth man was tall and dark skinned, with the sharp, angular features of someone from the Middle East. He would be Ahmed, the group's new leader.

The portal showed a familiar scene: white-clad Kugo security forces marching up the trail to the elemental shrine. They were almost to the entrance. Good, the tunnel's mouth would be a strong defensive position should any of the Spirit Eaters escape.

One of the original members, a reedy man with thinning blond hair, whose name Daisuke couldn't recall, spoke up, his voice quavering. "There're too many of them, Ahmed. We can't possibly win."

Ahmed fixed him with a withering glare. "Fool. They're fire spirit magic users and the orb is charged with water magic. That, combined with our own anti-spirit spells, will be more than enough to crush them. Don't tell me you're losing your courage now, when we're on the verge of total victory."

Ahmed aside, the other Spirit Eaters' faces made their fear obvious. Even when he'd been with them, the group hadn't been overly interested in direct confrontations. They were more the "sneaking around in the background and scrounging what they could" types. Basically human hyenas. A new leader had done little to stiffen their spines.

Good, he could use that.

Well done, Ruq. Be ready to strike when I say.

Ruq's eagerness to sting people to death came through their link loud and clear. It always left a bad taste in Daisuke's mouth, but Ruq was a demon after all.

Ahmed's face contorted with fury. He slammed his fist on the floor. "This is why you never accomplished anything before I took over! You're nothing but a bunch of weak, useless cowards! We're going to attack that shrine and crush those cursed spirit magic users before they can set up their defenses. And anyone who has a problem is welcome to try and take my place as leader."

He surged to his feet, his dark eyes blazing. To punctuate his threat, Ahmed reached into his tan robe and pulled out a blue orb that pulsed with light. He waved it in front of his followers' faces, the threat unsubtle.

Daisuke pushed through the store's front door and strode right toward the group. It was time to take Ahmed up on his offer. "I'll give it a try."

The Spirit Eaters whirled to face him, their expressions

slack with surprise. Ahmed's eyes narrowed, his lips curling back from his teeth in a snarl.

"Who the hell are you?" His knuckles were white as he grasped the orb.

Before Daisuke could reply, one of the original members, a woman with short blond hair, asked, "Daisuke? Is that you?"

"Long time no see. Looks like you lot have gotten into a bit of trouble since we parted company. I've been sent by my employer to deal with you," Daisuke said, his tone light. "And to retrieve the orb."

Ahmed's face twisted. "You're a fool to challenge us alone, boy. We'll bury you then claim the shrine's power for ourselves."

Daisuke smiled, a cold humorless expression that didn't reach his eyes. "You talk big, but your troops don't seem down for a fight. For old time's sake, I'll make you a deal," he said, glancing at the other members. "Help me take out Ahmed. Once I have the orb you can go back to scratching around ruins looking for lost magic."

Mutters broke out among the Spirit Eaters as nervous glances darted between Daisuke and Ahmed. The Egyptian wizard glared at his minions, his fury at their hesitation an almost visible haze in the air.

Daisuke seized on Ahmed's distraction.

Black lightning arced out from the staff toward Ahmed.

The spell crashed against a shimmering barrier of water that sprang up around the sorcerer, leaving him unscathed.

All hell broke loose.

Some of the Spirit Eaters bolted for the exits, desperate to escape the impending battle. Others hurled themselves at Daisuke, dark magic flaring to life in their hands.

Stupid of them.

He sidestepped a blast of necromantic energy before retaliating with a bolt of black lightning that dropped his nearest attacker in his tracks, the life completely burned out of him.

A second man screamed when Ruq drove his stinger into the man's neck. The imp's glee at killing came through their link loud and clear.

Daisuke ignored his familiar's fun and focused on Ahmed. He was the only true threat. The man had conjured a wall of churning water between himself and Daisuke.

Tentacles of liquid lashed out, forcing Daisuke to backpedal. A counter blast of lightning fizzled against the barrier.

"Pathetic!" Ahmed shouted from the safety of his barrier. "Did you think you could defeat me with such weak magic?"

Daisuke shifted tactics. He leveled the staff and opened a black disk under Ahmed's feet.

The wizard leapt back an instant before black lightning arced up.

Taking advantage of the distraction, Daisuke blew away the wall of water with a concussive blast.

Fully exposed, Ahmed's confidence vanished. He brandished the orb and a moment later a wall of ice appeared, blocking everything from one side of the building to the other.

Daisuke swallowed a curse. Before he could pursue, Ruq's warning hit his brain. *Watch out!*

He spun and swung the staff, smashing a woman in the side of the head as she tried to sneak up on him, her hands crackling with hellfire.

A burst of black lightning made sure she wouldn't threaten him again.

"Ruq, find Ahmed!"

He sensed his familiar growing further away. He might get lucky, but Daisuke wasn't counting on it. The Spirit Eaters with the will to fight had been dealt with, but the rest had scattered.

I circled the whole building, Master. No sign of him.

Daisuke swallowed a curse. "Okay, come back."

A minute later Ruq glided down from a hole in the ceiling. "He was quick. I didn't even catch a glimpse of which way he went. What now?"

Daisuke put the staff away and drew his knife. "Now we hunt down a stray."

When he reactivated the tracking spell it thankfully didn't point at any of the bodies. The brother, it seemed, had the good sense to flee.

"Can I sting him to death?" Ruq asked.

"No, at least not until I find out if he knows where Ahmed ran off to. If he's less than cooperative, well, we'll see."

Ruq rubbed his little hands together as if Daisuke had already given him permission.

CHAPTER SIXTEEN

Helena and Jinx made their way past the traffickers' warehouse. Aside from bloodstains, scorch marks, mangled metal, and a hint of brimstone, the area had been cleaned up nicely. Looked like it wouldn't take too long for them to get the docks back to one hundred percent. It was a bit of a surprise that no one was working on it today. Maybe the pending investigation was delaying things.

Helena didn't especially care about the state of the Odessa docks, but it was always nice to see things restored to their proper state. It felt like a victory of order over chaos.

She and Jinx had just left the police department behind after a second interview with Petruk. He was remarkably eager to help and directed them to a boat shack at the end of the dock where the smugglers' boat was hidden. He even provided the combination for the lock. It was a pity all the criminals she was forced to deal with weren't equally cooperative.

"Are you sure about this?" Jinx glanced over her shoulder

at the Black Sea. "The demon octopus is still out there along with the humanoid eels. A boat trip might not be the best idea."

Helena's lips pressed into a thin line. She wasn't all that excited about heading into open water either, but they'd run out of clues in Odessa. She wanted to wrap up the cult of Dagon thing before they turned their attention to Staryol. They'd need to take precautions before approaching a place that close to the radiation zone and she was content to put it off for as long as possible.

"You might be right, but I can't think of a better idea. Hopefully we can find some clues in the burned-out village."

"And not a bunch of hungry monsters," Jinx said.

"I'm okay with that too."

They reached the boat shack at the far end of the dock. It was nothing special, just a sturdy metal garage built over the water to provide shelter for the smugglers' boat. Dozens of identical buildings like it lined this section of the docks. If you didn't know who owned it, you'd never give the building a second look.

Helena punched the code into a lock built into the handle and the deadbolt whirred open. She sensed no life forces inside and sure enough when she flipped the light on no one was around.

What they did find was a sturdy, fifty-foot vessel moored against the dock. It was gray fiberglass with an enclosed pilot's station. She climbed aboard and checked belowdecks. Automatic rifles were stacked neatly in racks along one wall. Beyond them was the brig.

She wrinkled her nose when she opened the door. The stench of sweat and human misery still lingered. How many poor souls had been crammed in there over the years? Best not to think too hard about it.

Back up on deck, they went to the helm and found a state-of-the-art GPS system. She had no idea what most of the buttons did and was frankly uncertain how to turn it on.

Jinx peered over her shoulder at the GPS. "Do you know how to work this thing?"

"Not a clue, but if it's got a screen and buttons, Crystal will know how to run it." She got her phone out and pressed the number for Crystal's room at headquarters.

After three rings Crystal said, "Helena? Is everything okay? You don't usually call me directly."

"Everything is pretty much okay. I saw no reason to bother the boss with a tech support question. I've got a fancy-looking GPS unit here and I need it to tell me how to reach the last place this boat visited. Can you help me out?"

"Shouldn't be a problem. Snap a picture of the unit and send it to me."

Helena turned to Jinx. "Could you take a picture of the unit and send it to Crystal, please?"

Jinx beamed at her. "I can! Daisuke taught me how a little while before he left. Just a sec."

Helena swallowed her annoyance at the reminder of how close the two of them were and watched as Jinx got out her phone and carefully took a picture.

"Got it," Crystal said a few seconds later. "Okay, this looks like a pretty basic unit."

Helena stared at all the buttons and shook her head. Crystal thought this was basic? If that was true, she'd hate to see a complicated unit.

"First you need to turn it on," Crystal said. "Hit the button on the back right of the unit."

Helena found it and pressed. The GPS display lit up. After that it was a matter of clicking through a few menus and she had the route up and ready to go.

"Thanks, Crystal. You really saved our bacon."

"Glad I could help. If you need anything else, I'll be here."

Helena disconnected and turned her focus to the helm, once again feeling out of her depth. She'd never driven anything bigger than a jet ski. How was she supposed to handle this thing? Jinx looked equally clueless.

"Can you drive a boat?" Jinx asked.

"No, you?"

Jinx shook her head. "Do you think Mr. Borys might?"

Helena slapped her forehead. How had she not thought of that? Well, whatever. She fired off a quick text.

Borys replied that he was on his way.

Minutes later, heavy footsteps announced his arrival. Borys stomped down the dock and climbed into the boat. He took one look at the helm and nodded. "No problem. Our destination is programed into the GPS, yes?"

Helena nodded. "How do you know how to drive a boat?"

"Two years in the river patrol." Borys pressed a button and the garage door slid up out of sight. "Untie us, please."

Jinx hurried over to the rope connecting them to the dock and yanked it free. "Okay."

Borys hit the ignition, pushed a lever forward, and they were on their way.

Helena braced herself against the railing as they picked up speed. She had no idea how far they had to go, but it was a nice day for a boat ride. Assuming the demon octopus didn't show up.

Happily it didn't and two hours later the island she assumed was their destination appeared ahead of them. As they drew closer, the island resolved into a jagged coastline. The charred remains of a village were nestled in a little cove with a simple dock jutting out into the sea.

Another boat, smaller than theirs by about half, bobbed gently at the dock. It was a fishing boat with nets hanging on either side. A cluster of five men were picking their way through the rubble. What they were looking for she couldn't begin to imagine.

One figure stood apart from the rest, swathed in dark robes, the hood pulled up to shade his face. Even at this distance, Helena could feel the corruption around him. He wasn't that impressive compared to some of the hellpriests she'd fought, but she'd still prefer to avoid a battle with him.

Beside her, Jinx tensed. "Uh-oh. I don't like the feel of this."

"Me either. I didn't expect to find a hellpriest here."

"How do you want to handle it?"

Helena considered their options. "If he isn't looking for a fight, this might work to our advantage. I can't think of anyone better to tell us what's going on around here."

Jinx frowned. "That sounds optimistic, but okay."

Borys guided them right up to the dock opposite the fishing boat. One of the men strode over and Helena tossed him a rope. He caught it and tied them to the dock.

"Thanks," Helena said.

He didn't speak, but did offer a polite nod. Probably didn't understand English. Hardly a surprise given how remote these islands were.

She turned back to Borys. "Stay here. We shouldn't be too long."

He offered a thumbs-up instead of an argument which suited Helena very well. She and Jinx hopped down to the dock and strode right to the hellpriest who watched them from the shadows of his hood.

Helena hadn't dealt with many hellpriests, but she knew enough not to show him any fear. A moment of weakness might be the end of her or at least an end to any hope for a pleasant conversation.

"Can we talk?" she asked. "About what happened here?"

"Who are you?" His voice was as deep and dark as his hood and his English surprisingly clear. "Not the ones who've been raiding our villages."

Helena shook her head. "No, we're working with the Odessa police to investigate the situation. We've dealt with the human traffickers and rescued a number of survivors. Not all of them unfortunately, but a dozen at least."

The hellpriest paused, silently thinking. At last he said, "Follow me, away from the others."

Helena and Jinx walked along with the hellpriest as he led them away from his companions to a spot where they could speak without being overheard. The stink of smoke and death lingered in the ruined village. It was a different sort of unpleasant from the room under the warehouse. Helena had to fight the urge to cover her nose.

"Do you worship Dagon?" Helena asked. "One of the women had a mark and the magic felt like his. The demon octopus was a hint as well."

The hellpriest threw his hood back, revealing a pale but surprisingly handsome face and frowned. "The master is called the Lord of the Ocean here."

"Okay. But whatever he's called, why didn't he protect these villages? Aren't they filled with his worshippers?"

The hellpriest's frown deepened. "There are many islands and the master has only so many servants. We cannot be everywhere at once. We tried to eliminate the threat at its source, but some new magic prevented us from doing so."

"The barrier has been destroyed along with the human traffickers. Your people will be safe now, at least from them."

The hellpriest narrowed his cold blue eyes. "And you did all this out of the goodness of your heart?"

Helena refused to look away. "I did what was necessary to protect people. I had no idea the cult of Dagon was involved until the octopus attacked."

"What will you do now?" the hellpriest asked. "Keep our people prisoner?"

"No," Helena said. "They're free to do as they please. If they wish to return to the islands, no one will stop them."

"This is surprising," the hellpriest said. "Normally busy-bodies like you would do all they could to keep our people from returning."

Helena smiled. "Normally a hellpriest would attack us on sight in the hopes of cutting our hearts out as an offering to their master. If my behavior is strange, then so is yours."

"The master has chosen a different way here. It has worked well for decades, until the outsiders came and attacked us."

Helena had serious doubts that Dagon had suddenly taken a magnanimous turn in philosophy but this wasn't the time to discuss it. "Do you know what drew their attention to your settlements?"

"No. We never captured one of the raiders alive. If you've dealt with them, we can return to the old ways."

"As long as your ways don't include attacking shipping or the Odessa docks, I'm all for it. If we have nothing left to discuss, we'll be on our way. I appreciate your willingness to talk things through peacefully."

"It is well. Travel safely."

As Helena and Jinx made their way back to the boat Jinx asked, "Did you think it was going to go this way?"

"Nothing that's happened since the attack on the docks has gone the way I expected. Most of it has gone better and I don't trust that for a second."

They climbed into the boat and Helena untied it. Without a word, Borys started the engine and pulled away from the dock. Helena looked back at the hellpriest who was watching them as they left. She wasn't sure what to make of the man. He was both weaker and saner than any hellpriest she'd ever encountered. No doubt those two things were related.

Jinx moved over beside her. "Did we do the right thing, leaving him alive? I doubt Daisuke would've."

"Daisuke has a somewhat extreme personality when it comes to these sorts of things. He's also stronger than us which makes violence a more successful option for him." Helena sighed. "I think we made the best decision we could."

"I guess. It's not like we don't know where to find him if he starts making trouble later."

Helena hoped it wouldn't come to that though she knew it might. For better or worse matters in the Black Sea were settled for the moment. It was time to turn their attention to Staryol.

CHAPTER SEVENTEEN

Daisuke stepped out of the gutted store and checked the tracking spell before turning down the street. He kept the dagger flat against his forearm so no one would notice it at a glance. In a modern Japanese city, a man walking around carrying a blood-covered dagger would draw attention he didn't want.

It didn't matter which position he held the dagger in. As long as the magic was active it would guide him to the dead woman's brother. He couldn't have gotten far given the brevity of the battle.

Daisuke followed the magic deeper into the city. It wasn't even noon yet, but he felt like he'd been on the hunt for way longer. Time always ran funny when he was in the middle of a mission. Sometimes a minute felt like an hour and vice versa.

The tracking spell tugged him down another street. The vibration was getting stronger. Not much farther now.

A little ways on he spotted a lonely bus stop. No one was waiting for a ride thank goodness. Beside a covered bench was a public restroom. Daisuke sensed only a single life form inside. Perfect.

He shouldered open the door and eyed the row of three stalls. His target was hiding in the farthest one from the door. Daisuke knocked.

"Occupied!"

"I know it's occupied. I don't need to take a leak but if you keep me waiting out here, I'm going to get even more ticked off. Now open up."

A whimper was followed by shuffling. The latch clicked and the stall door swung inward.

The man cowering inside looked pathetic. Tear-streaked face, rumpled robe, not a shred of dignity. Daisuke shook his head. This guy was giving wizards a bad name.

"P-please, don't kill me. I didn't even want to come to Japan, Ahmed insisted. He said we'd find our destiny here. I don't think getting wiped out was what he had in mind."

Daisuke sighed. This was too pathetic. "Will you relax? Tell me what I want to know and you and the others smart enough to run can go back to Europe. Live a quiet life and never cause me any trouble again."

"Absolutely, what can I tell you?"

"To start with, where did Ahmed run off to?"

"I... I don't know. The plan was to go from the store to the shrine."

"There's no way you were all holing up in that gutted store without supplies or beds."

"We were staying at a motel until this morning, but we checked out and left nothing behind. He has no reason to go back."

Daisuke's magic confirmed the truth of his words. Talk about inconvenient.

"Tell me about the orb."

"Ahmed is obsessed with it. He stole it from a collector in Cairo. He said we could use it to claim the spirits' magic and use it for ourselves. It worked too. Before he sensed the shrine open, we attacked a water spirit temple in the desert. The orb sucked the magic right out of the guardian spirit and killed it. It was amazing."

"Okay. What else?"

"The orb has a single weakness. It can only hold one type of elemental energy at a time. You have to drain it before you can absorb something else."

Daisuke grimaced. That weakness might be a strength right now since only fire magic users were defending the shrine.

"Why are you trying to stop us?" the man asked. "You hated the spirits more than any of us when you were a member. If you'd stayed, you could've been our leader and we wouldn't have listened to Ahmed."

"I was young and full of resentment." Daisuke wasn't sure why he bothered to explain himself, but he felt like he owed them something as former comrades. "My hatred helped me cope with other things. Though I still have no use for them, my hatred of the spirits has cooled. Anyway, assuming this had worked out, what was the end game?"

"Ahmed wanted to establish a base for us in the Sinai Peninsula. He was obsessed with the area, though I have no idea why. It's mostly empty desert and terrorists."

Daisuke knew next to nothing about the Middle East and for now it didn't matter. Figuring this stuff out was the boss's job. He had a hunt to finish. If Ahmed was this determined, no way would he give up without taking a shot at the spirit shrine. Having seen the orb's power, Daisuke wasn't optimistic about the clan's ability to stop him.

Setting up a trap in the park might be his best bet; catch him before he reached the shrine.

"What happens now?" the wizard asked.

"You gather up the others and leave Japan. Disappear and don't let me hear about you again. As long as you don't cause any trouble, you'll all be fine."

The man's eyes widened. "You're letting us go?"

"We were allies once. The magic I learned from you has come in handy on several occasions. Consider this my way of saying thank you for back then. Now get lost before I change my mind."

He hesitated then asked, "My sister, she's dead, isn't she?"

Daisuke nodded. "I'm sorry."

The man sighed. "Me too. She was a true believer. She imagined Ahmed would lead us to glory. The sister I knew died when he took over the Spirit Eaters. Ahmed's nuts, Daisuke. You'll be doing the world a favor if you kill him."

With that the man scurried away, leaving the bathroom quickly behind.

"I can't believe you let him live," Ruq said.

Daisuke shrugged. "He was no threat and I'm not inclined to murder harmless weaklings."

"How nice of you," Ruq said. "And Ahmed? You think we can catch him before he reaches the shrine?"

"I'm not optimistic, but I mean to try. First I need to warn Natsumi. That orb could cause her and the others real trouble."

Natsumi paced off to one side of the tunnel entrance. Behind her the elemental shrine was abuzz with activity. Kugo security forces scrambled around as they rushed to prepare defensive positions for an attack none of them were sure would come.

She clenched her fists, grimaced, and forced herself to relax. Her offer to help had been met with a curt order to stay out of the adults' way. Just like that they sidelined her, and after she sounded the alarm. Of course she couldn't be too surprised. Defying Uncle Yoshikazu's orders never ended well for anyone, but that didn't make it any less frustrating.

Her phone buzzed, distracting her from her silent rant. She pulled it out of her pocket. Daisuke, hopefully he had good news. "What's up?"

"I dealt with most of the Spirit Eaters, but their leader got away. I suspect he's heading straight for the shrine."

"One guy is planning to take on the clan? Is he crazy?"

"Yes, but that's another issue altogether. The artifact he stole is way stronger than I expected. I'll intercept him if I can, but there are no guarantees. You need to warn whoever's in charge."

"I will. Thanks, Daisuke." She hung up and turned to scan the shrine, looking for her cousin Uki.

Natsumi spotted her a moment later shouting orders while pointing at something she didn't like. Uki was eight years older than Natsumi and considered something of a rising star in the clan. She'd never failed a mission and that was no doubt why Uncle Yoshikazu had sent her to oversee security at the shrine.

For some reason she also thoroughly disliked Natsumi.

"Cousin Uki," Natsumi said when she got close. "I've got news."

Uki whirled around, her eyes flashing. "What part of stay out of the way did you misunderstand? The grown-ups have work to do."

Biting back a nasty retort, Natsumi said, "Daisuke called. He took out most of the group, but the leader escaped. He says the artifact is more powerful than he first thought. Just thought you should know."

"I don't care how powerful his artifact is, we can handle one wizard."

Natsumi's temper flared. "Yeah? Did you forget what one guy with an artifact did to us earlier this summer? How long did it take you to fully recover?"

Uki snarled. "Enough! That was different. He took us by surprise. I appreciate the warning, now make yourself scarce."

Stubborn, arrogant idiot. Natsumi stalked off toward the fire temple. How could Uki not see that this was exactly the same as what happened last time? The Viking didn't take them by surprise, he overpowered them. And only a fool would think it couldn't happen again.

As she approached the white stone temple, she spotted Miles sitting on the steps. He seemed perfectly at ease as he took in the hubbub. Maybe he had the right idea. If Uki didn't want their help, why worry about her?

She smiled, now she was thinking like Daisuke.

"Natsumi," Miles said when she was closer. "You look upset."

"Daisuke called with a warning, but Uki won't take me seriously. Her ego won't let her. I'm afraid it's going to get people killed."

He patted the steps beside him and she sat, suddenly tired beyond words.

"What did he say?" Miles asked.

Natsumi repeated Daisuke's message. "One guy or not, if he was strong enough to escape Daisuke, we can't take him lightly."

"Indeed, but you can't control what others choose to do. Instead you can decide where and how you will face the enemy should he arrive."

She didn't have to think for long. There was only one place to make her stand, with her father.

Determination renewed, Natsumi stood. "Thanks, Miles."

She strode toward the spell circle where her father waited, helpless, as his arm recovered.

Natsumi was halfway to her destination when an explosion rocked the cavern. She stumbled, then caught herself. Billowing steam obscured her view of the tunnel entrance, but flashes of flame pierced the haze making it clear her relatives had engaged the intruder.

She snatched out her phone and sent a quick text to Daisuke. *He's here. Hurry!*

That done she ran on, anxious to reach her father. She found him unharmed and on his feet, watching the distant battle. "Dad! Are you okay?"

He didn't look away. "I'm fine. I—"

Before he could say anything else, the haze faded away revealing a dark-robed figure with bronze, Middle Eastern features. He thrust a blue orb before him, and massive icicles erupted out of it, hammering against the Kugos' defenses. The air sizzled as they melted against the fiery barriers.

Natsumi clenched her fists. She wanted to lend a hand, but didn't dare attack indiscriminately lest she be more hinderance than help.

"Stay calm," her father said. "Wait for an opening."

She nodded, his voice steadying her nerves.

The orb's glow began to fade. Was Ahmed's power waning?

The Kugo wizards seemed to think so. As one they hurled a massive wave of fire at Ahmed.

Natsumi's breath caught. This was it.

Or so she believed.

The flames struck the now-dull orb and were sucked in. It flared a brilliant, angry red as it absorbed their magic. Ahmed emerged without so much as a scorched thread on his robe.

Bad as the situation was, things could've been worse. At least the stolen fire magic couldn't harm the Kugo wizards.

Whatever relief she felt shattered as Ahmed attacked with magic of his own. Tendrils of dark energy lashed out, laying wizards low or sending them flying into the cavern walls. Every counterspell was absorbed harmlessly by the orb.

Ahmed strode through the now-silent cavern toward the fire temple.

She couldn't let him claim the spirits' power. If she could just hold out until Daisuke got here. Heart racing, Natsumi sprinted after him.

"Ahmed!" She launched herself into a flying kick.

And slammed into an invisible barrier for her trouble. Pain shot up her leg and a moment later she was hurled backward.

Natsumi hit the ground hard, the impact driving the air from her lungs.

Gasping, she struggled to rise. A shadow fell over her. Ahmed loomed above her, dark energy crackling around his fist.

"Foolish girl, you cannot stop me."

This was it. She was going to die.

"I will be your opponent now." Miles stepped forward, drawing Ahmed's attention away from Natsumi.

Unable to believe her luck, Natsumi scrambled to her feet. She wanted to help Miles, but as had been made clear a moment ago, she was no match for Ahmed.

The two wizards faced off, ether crackling between them. The air hummed with the force of it.

"You're no Kugo," Ahmed said. "Why die to protect the spirits' power?"

"The spirits have been kind enough to allow me to stay here for a time. I can't very well repay their kindness with betrayal. Can I convince you to walk away?"

"No," Ahmed said. "I will claim the spirits' power or die trying."

"What a waste." Miles pointed and a brown disk appeared in the air. A humanoid figure made of solid stone stomped out and stalked toward Ahmed.

"You think you can beat me with a spirit?" Ahmed's disgust came through loud and clear.

An instant later his eyes turned blood red and the earth elemental roared in pain. From the look on his face, Miles wasn't faring that well either. He must be suffering through his connection to the elemental.

Natsumi recognized the spell Ahmed was using. It was the same one Daisuke cast when they fought their duel. What did he call it, Crimson Haze? The anti-spirit magic was tearing the elemental apart.

She had to do something, but the orb would absorb any magic she used and the barrier would protect him from physical attacks.

She was still debating what to do when a black disk

appeared under Ahmed's feet. Black lightning arced up into his body. He spasmed and writhed and the magic shredded his life force until he collapsed into a steaming heap.

From out of nowhere Daisuke appeared. He had his staff in hand and a grim scowl on his face.

The elemental vanished and Miles blew out a long breath. "Took you long enough, son."

Daisuke bent and collected the orb from Ahmed's dead hand. While he was down there he snapped a picture of the man's face with his phone. "I got here as quickly as I could. You sensed my presence, right? That's why you tricked him into using Crimson Haze as a distraction."

"You give me too much credit."

Daisuke's eyes narrowed. "Maybe. Find anything?"

While they were talking Ruq had been rifling through Ahmed's pockets. "No, he's broke and empty handed."

The imp flew up on Daisuke's shoulder and turned into a rat.

"What now?" Natsumi asked. "Is it over?"

"For the moment," Daisuke said. "Now that the shrine has been revealed, you'll need to protect it, but the Spirit Eaters won't be a problem anymore. I also checked the cousins on my way in. They're in rough shape, but no one died."

Natsumi let out a breath. "Thank the spirits."

"Just them?" Daisuke asked.

Natsumi grinned. "Thank you, too."

He nodded. "That's better. I'll leave the cleanup to you two. I need to get back to Zurich. The sooner the orb is in the vault, the happier I'll be."

"See you soon, son," Miles said.

Daisuke made no comment. A sappy father-son moment wasn't in the cards today or likely ever.

With a backward wave, Daisuke stepped into the nearest shadow and vanished.

"Not much for goodbyes, is he?" Miles asked.

"No. Lucky for us, last-minute rescues are more his thing. I need to call Uncle Yoshikazu. Are you okay?"

Miles nodded. "A little sore, but otherwise fine. Do what you must. I'll check on the survivors. I have a knack for healing magic."

Miles walked off, leaving her alone. Natsumi took a deep, steadying breath. Somehow everyone had survived. It seemed like a miracle, but she wasn't about to question it.

She dug out her phone and called home. Whatever came next, she was happy it wasn't up to her to sort out.

CHAPTER EIGHTEEN

Daisuke appeared out of a shadow behind Arcane Books and Trinkets. He took a deep breath of cool Zurich air. It was good to be home, no doubt about that. He unlocked the back door and turned toward the boss's office. He was so distracted thinking about what happened in Japan that he nearly ran Vixen over. She was dressed in a green knee-length dress that looked wonderful with her red hair.

It was good to see the former assassin up and moving around. She'd only been released from the medical room a couple days before he left for Japan and had moved in with Jinx until they could set her up in a place of her own.

"Hey," Daisuke said. "How are you doing?"

She offered a stunning smile. "I'm good, though I tire out faster than I'd like. I'm helping in the shop today, learning the ropes before I start full time. The job's easier than I feared."

"After being an assassin for a demon cult, I imagine retail isn't much of a challenge."

"All my memories from that time are hazy and getting hazier by the day. It's like the spirit took them away with her when she was destroyed. I'm not complaining!" Vixen hastened to add. "The few memories I have from those days make it clear the loss of the others is a gift, not a curse."

"I never thought you were complaining. I need to check in, but, assuming I don't have to head right back out, what do you say we have dinner tonight?"

She brightened. "I'd love to. It's kind of lonely in Jinx's apartment when she's gone."

"Great, I know the perfect place. They serve fantastic cheesecake. I'll pick you up after the shop closes. See you later."

He let Vixen return to work and continued on to the boss's office. After a quick knock she said, "Come in."

Daisuke went inside and found the office surprisingly free of tobacco smoke. The boss was seated behind her desk, studying a pile of papers. He wasn't sure if she was trying to make sense of them or make them disappear.

She looked up and waved him into his usual chair. "How'd it go?"

Daisuke put the orb on her desk. "No one died except the people I wanted dead and as you can see, I got the artifact. All in all, a good result. On the less encouraging side, I've got a bunch more questions, the most pressing of which being, what did Ahmed intend to do with the orb's power."

"Maybe you'd better give me a full report."

Daisuke obliged. It was strange how comfortable it was being honest with her. The boss might be the only person he felt so at ease with.

Hey!

I don't have to be honest with you, we share our thoughts. That doesn't count. I couldn't lie to you if I wanted to.

"I'm surprised you let some of them go," she said when he finished his report.

"Those clowns are no threat to anyone. They'll go back to poking around picked-over ruins and hunting weak spirits. I made it clear what would happen if they did anything else. I'm more interested in Ahmed's obsession with the Sinai. Do we have any resources in the area?"

"No, but Anatoly was in Egypt for six months, he might've heard something. You can ask him when you reach Istanbul."

"Come again?"

"I sent him to scout out the situation with the death glider. It was going to be Helena and Jinx's next mission, but since you're back, you can deal with it. Shouldn't be a problem. Once that's cleaned up, you and Anatoly can head back to Egypt and see what you can learn."

"Right." Daisuke wasn't thrilled about going right back out on another mission, but the trip to Japan had been a personal thing rather than Circle business so he couldn't complain. "What do you want me to do with the orb?"

"In the vault."

Exactly what he expected her to say. "Do you want me to drain it first or leave it as is?"

She frowned. "Might as well drain it. I doubt anything would happen in the vault, but why take chances? You leave in the morning. Wait, have you been to Istanbul?"

"Once, years ago. I shouldn't have any trouble reaching it via the shadow paths. Where do I meet Anatoly?"

"Good question. I'll contact him then send you the details.

Rest up. Japan ended up being a bigger thing than I expected."

"You and me both. I wonder if there are more elemental shrines."

"I've never heard of one," she said. "But then again, I hadn't heard of the one in Japan. The truth is, this world has so many mysteries I doubt even an immortal like me could learn the truth of them all."

Daisuke stood and collected the orb. "I don't find that terribly reassuring, Boss. See you later."

He had a few hours before Vixen got off work. Plenty of time to drain the orb and lock it down in the vault. Whatever was waiting for him in Istanbul, he planned to enjoy tonight.

CHAPTER NINETEEN

The pickup Helena rented bounced and rattled down the dirt road to Staryol. The heavy springs didn't provide the nicest ride, but at least she wasn't worried about getting stuck. It was easy to see that no one did much in the way of maintenance out here. They'd left Ukraine behind an hour ago and were now in unclaimed territory.

Beside her, Jinx gripped the passenger-side handle so tightly her knuckles were white against the cracked leather. Dust clouds billowed behind them, obscuring their path back.

"How's the Geiger counter look?" Helena asked. They'd bought the device before leaving Odessa and any moment she expected it to start buzzing.

"The little arrow is barely moving and hasn't come close to leaving the green area. I think we're still okay. How much farther to Staryol?" Jinx asked.

"I'm not sure, but it can't be much further." Helena tried

her best to sound optimistic. "Maybe another fifteen minutes."

Jinx made no comment about her guess which Helena appreciated. The road twisted and turned ahead of them, the scenery unchanging. They passed rocky outcrops, skeletal trees, and damn little else. She hadn't seen a bird or sensed the presence of an animal in far too long. It was more lifeless out here than in the Outback.

Finally, half an hour later, they crested a small hill. At the base of it was the dingiest little town Helena had ever seen. It was little more than a collection of rundown houses, their roofs sagging and the paint, what remained of it, peeling like a sunburned surfer. Helena pulled the truck to a stop on the roadside about twenty yards from the nearest building.

While the dust settled, she said, "We'll walk in for a closer look. Let's not do anything aggressive unless we're attacked."

"Do you want me to summon some shadows just in case?" Jinx asked.

"No, Sava might notice them and think we're looking for a fight."

"Are we not looking for a fight? This guy seems pretty evil, assuming everything we've been told is true."

"Exactly, assuming it's true. That's the bit we're here to confirm. I also want to get an idea of how strong he is. Starting an unnecessary fight you might not be able to win isn't wise, despite what Daisuke thinks. Come on." She stepped out of the truck, her shoes crunching on the gravel as she walked to the edge of the road.

Jinx followed, Geiger counter in hand.

They strode down the road through the town. Nothing moved and no one put in an appearance. Worst of all, she sensed no life forces. The whole setup was creepy as hell.

"Nothing but old houses," Helena muttered. "Where is everyone?"

Jinx shook her head, but Helena hadn't expected an answer. Instead she went to the nearest house and knocked. She waited, focusing hard and still sensing no life inside.

She knocked again, harder this time. Nothing.

They moved from house to house, every knock met with silence. Each home was as empty and lifeless as the next. At the sixth one Helena crossed her arms.

"Knocking is getting us nowhere. Let's take a look inside."

"Is that okay?" Jinx asked.

Helena looked all around. "Who's going to complain?"

She inserted a bit of ether into the lock and formed it into a key. The lock clicked and she pushed the door open. Dust motes filled the air along with the dry, musty smell of a house that's been closed up for too long.

No way was anyone living in this place. They searched the entire house and found nothing but rotten furniture a century out of style.

They left the house and Helena frowned. It was looking more and more like this place was a bust. She was about to suggest leaving when a faint vibration ran through the ether. A closer look confirmed something corrupt was headed their way.

"Do you feel that?" Jinx asked.

"Yup. Company's coming."

A group of people shuffled toward them from every direction, their movements jerky and uncoordinated. Their faces were sunken and their eyes glowed with a dull crimson light. A faint aura of corruption surrounded them. Thralls, weak ones to be sure, but she counted over a hundred of them. Way too many for Jinx and her to handle.

Jinx moved to stand back-to-back with her. "This isn't good."

The thralls surrounded them, then stopped about ten feet away. They made no aggressive moves, seeming content to simply stand and stare.

Helena's nerves were stretched tight. What were they waiting for? Not that she was eager for a fight with this many thralls, regardless of their lack of power.

The answer to her question arrived a minute later when the thralls parted and a man strode through the gap. He wore a bizarre outfit made of black leather with cut outs that allowed strips of barbed wire to run through them. Every time he moved, the spikes dug into his flesh. Blood oozed from countless wounds, but he didn't seem troubled.

He stopped a few feet from Helena and Jinx. "I am Sava Rude. Do you two lovely ladies have business with me?"

Helena's heart lurched. This close, the corruption clinging to him was overwhelming. She'd never encountered anyone so strong.

She licked her dry lips, trying in vain to work some moisture up. "Petruk mentioned your name. He said you created the barrier that protected their warehouse from Dagon's monsters. We thought doing something similar with transport ships might protect them as well."

Helena was careful to word her statement to make sure it included no lies.

Sava grinned. "Is that so? Well then, let's discuss it in my workshop, shall we?"

Helena forced a smile. "Thank you for your hospitality, but if you can give us an idea of the price and time required to erect such a barrier, that should be sufficient for now. If our employers are interested, we can return to finalize the arrangements."

Sava cocked his head, studying her with eyes that burned red. "As you wish. For a ship the size of a large cargo vessel, I would require a payment of half a million Euros. It would also require a group of ten sacrifices whose suffering would power the barrier. I can begin as soon as you provide the payment and sacrifices. The process will take a single day. It would be best if the vessel had a private room to hold the people."

Helena nodded, careful to keep her disgust from showing. "Thank you for the explanation. We'll relay the details to our employer and be in touch."

Sava gestured and the wall of thralls parted, opening a path for Helena and Jinx. Helena offered a shallow bow and hurried toward the truck, Jinx a step behind. She didn't dare look back.

They made it to the vehicle safe and sound. As soon as the doors closed, Jinx slumped in her seat. "Wow. He was crazy strong. A hellpriest of Golmol I'd say."

"Yes, and a wizard too. That's an unusual combination. Wizards seldom also worship a demon lord. We're definitely going to need backup for this."

"I can't figure out why he let us go," Jinx said. "He had us dead to rights."

Helena started the engine with shaking hands. "Arrogance, I'm sure. He figured even if we came back with ill intentions, we'd be no match for him. It's one of the most common failings of demon worshippers. Daisuke should be back by now. The three of us ought to be enough to take him down."

Jinx looked back as Helena pulled onto the road. "I hope so."

CHAPTER TWENTY

The incessant ringing of his cellphone dragged Daisuke awake. He glanced around his bedroom, momentarily disoriented. He'd had a nice dinner with Vixen but when he invited her back here she'd begged off, not wanting to do anything that might hurt Jinx's feelings. She seemed to be under the impression he had a more serious relationship with Jinx than he did.

He groaned and snatched the phone off his nightstand. "Yeah, Boss."

"Change of plans. I need you in Odessa ASAP. Helena and Jinx ran into a powerful hellpriest and Helena didn't think they could handle him on their own."

"Right, okay." The boss's anxiety had finished waking him up. "I've never been to Odessa, but I've visited Kiev. I can fly the rest of the way."

"Good. They're waiting for you." She paused then added, "Be careful, Daisuke. I have a bad feeling about this one."

"When's the last time you had a good feeling about a

mission?" He tossed the covers aside. "I'll head out after breakfast. Send me the details."

He ended the call, rolled out of bed, and started getting dressed. A hellpriest strong enough to balk Helena and Jinx was nothing to sneeze at. An email arrived as he pulled his shoes on. The hellpriest served Golmol. That was rare. Daisuke had never fought one before.

Ruq crawled out of the covers in rat form and Daisuke asked, "What do you know about Golmol's hellpriests?"

"They're into pain and their boss is consistently lagging in the game of souls. It's hard to tempt people with promises of eternal torture even when you're the one dishing it out. It's amazing he finds as many hellpriests as he does."

"Thank you, I feel much more enlightened now. How about we split a dozen doughnuts before we go?"

"Get your own dozen," Ruq said.

That wasn't the worst idea Daisuke had ever heard. He grinned and set out for Stein's Bakery. No one wanted to face a hellpriest on an empty stomach.

Once his belly was full of carbs, Daisuke made the shadow walk to Kiev then the hour-long flight to Odessa. He landed in a half-full parking lot and released his invisibility spell.

Daisuke looked around at the dreary gray skyscrapers and sighed. It wasn't the ugliest city he'd ever visited, but it did leave something to be desired from an architectural perspective.

He punched in Helena's number and a few rings later she asked, "Where are you?"

"A parking lot in central Odessa." He heard the tension in her voice. It was rare for Helena to let that show. "Where are you?"

"Jinx and I are staying at the Yalta Hotel. Number seven on the fourth floor."

"Got it. I'll catch a cab."

The ride across town didn't take long and soon the cab pulled up in front of the Yalta Hotel. The gray slab of concrete was about as inviting as a morgue. But as long as it had beds and a bathroom it would do the job. He'd stayed in worse places while on a job.

"What a dump," Ruq muttered from his perch on Daisuke's shoulder. He was invisible at the moment since having a rat on display was the sort of thing that drew funny looks.

Daisuke didn't argue as he strode through the completely ordinary lobby and took the elevator up to the fourth floor. When he found Helena's room he knocked.

The door opened immediately, revealing a frazzled but still beautiful Helena. "Hey, the boss made it sound like you guys were in a tough spot."

"That's putting it mildly," Helena said. "Come in."

She moved aside and Daisuke went into the room. A moment later Jinx hopped off her bed and hugged him. "I missed you."

He smiled. "Likewise. Vixen says hi. She'll be starting at the store as soon as she finishes her training."

"I'm excited for her."

Helena cleared her throat and Daisuke reluctantly let Jinx go. They sat on the lumpy beds, Helena and Jinx facing him.

"If we could focus on the matter at hand," Helena said.

"I'm totally focused. The boss gave me the gist of the situation, but why don't you walk me through it step by step."

Helena obliged and the story didn't get any more pleasant with additional details.

When she finished Daisuke said, "So you ran into two hellpriests on a mission that was supposed to be just eliminating a minor demon? And the boss says I have bad luck. A bunch of weak thralls won't be a problem. If you two can keep them off me, I'll focus on the hellpriest. Depending on how that goes, I can help you finish the thralls or you can help me finish the hellpriest. What do you think?"

"Sounds reasonable to me," Helena said. "Though I doubt it'll go as smoothly as you make it sound. We'll have to drive back to Staryol. Flying will leave us too drained. If we leave now, we can camp for the night on this side of the border then approach at first light."

Daisuke barely opened his mouth to agree when Helena's phone rang. She snatched it up and frowned. "It's Rostolov."

She hit the speaker button. "Helena, something's happened at the hospital. It's a massacre. The survivors from the trafficking ring, the staff, the officers on guard duty, they're all dead. Butchered. Can you come?"

Helena hesitated, seeming uncertain about her response. When she looked at Daisuke he nodded. "Yes, we can take a look."

"I hoped you'd say that. Borys is already on his way."

They left the hotel room and went back downstairs to wait. Daisuke paced on the sidewalk as he watched for their ride.

"Why'd you tell me to agree?" Helena asked. "I feel bad for them, but solving murders, even horrific ones, isn't our mission."

Daisuke stopped and turned to face her. "Think about it. A few hours after your meeting with Sava the survivors are killed. No way that's a coincidence. If he's got some magic capable of wiping out an entire hospital floor from hundreds of miles away, we need to figure out how it works. Preferably before he uses it against us."

Helena blanched. "Do you think our visit triggered the attack?"

"No way to say for sure. Maybe he was just covering his bases. For that matter it might've been Dagon's hellpriest who sent whatever did this. We need to confirm the source as much as anything."

"I can't imagine Dagon's hellpriest would do that. He seemed to genuinely want them returned safe and sound," Jinx said.

Daisuke couldn't imagine any hellpriest caring about anyone's wellbeing other than their own, but he did find Jinx's optimism adorable.

A tan sedan pulled up to the curb, cutting off the conversation.

Daisuke slid into the passenger's seat while the ladies got in the back. The driver shot him a silent look.

"He's with us." Helena slammed the door shut. "Let's go."

Borys pulled away from the hotel without comment. Daisuke found himself impressed. Most people would be pelting him with questions by now. He appreciated not having to refuse to answer.

It didn't take long to reach the hospital. The place was nicer than Helena's hotel. A cop in a rumpled suit stood at the entrance, his face grim and exhausted. Daisuke held back, content to let Helena take the lead for the moment.

"I appreciate you coming," said the cop—Rostolov, Daisuke assumed. "Who's your friend?"

"Sergeant Rostolov, let me introduce you to our colleague, Daisuke Kugo. He came in to help us deal with

Sava Rude. As long as he's here, I thought an extra pair of eyes wouldn't hurt anything."

"I certainly won't complain about more help." Rostolov held out his hand and Daisuke shook it. "We're in a real mess here. Follow me."

They fell in behind Rostolov, who led the way into the hospital. The front desk was manned by a pair of cute nurses dressed in blue scrubs. Both of them glanced up and quickly away as the group passed. Looked like they'd heard about what happened upstairs.

A brief elevator ride took them to the floor in question. A chime sounded and the doors slid open.

The first thing that caught Daisuke's eye was the red streaks of blood running down the halls. Blood had splattered the walls and the stink of it was thick enough to choke on. Rostolov stepped out but didn't go far. "Everything is exactly as the officers found it. I thought it best to let you have a look before forensics."

"Good call," Daisuke said. "We'll see what we can figure out."

He led the way down the hall, peeking into each room as they passed and finding nothing but mutilated bodies. Whoever or whatever killed them hadn't been gentle.

"This is…" Jinx didn't finish and she didn't have to. He knew what she was thinking.

Daisuke gave her hand a squeeze then asked, "Where was the woman with Dagon's mark?"

"End of the hall," Helena said, her voice tight.

He quickened his pace. A cop lay dead and eviscerated in front of the door. Daisuke grimaced and stepped over him. Inside, a dead woman lay in the bed, her legs tangled in blood-soaked sheets. She hadn't died instantly and her head was intact. Good, he might be able to extract some information.

"I'm going to question her," Daisuke said. "Would you two mind checking the rest of the floor?"

"You're not going to bind her soul like you did Remi's." Helena made it a statement, not a question.

"No, you have to be present at the moment of death to do that. Her soul has already gone to whatever resting place it's earned. I'm going to extract her final memories from her brain. She must've gotten a look at whatever did this. You can stay and watch if you want, but the spell can be unsettling."

"No, we'll leave you to it." Helena hastened to withdraw, taking Jinx with her.

That was just as well. Proper necromancy had an aura about it that most people found uncomfortable. Daisuke had gotten used to it over the years.

"Okay, young lady, show me what did this to you."

Ether surged out of him and sank into her head. A moment later he gestured, pulling an image back out through her eyes. A looming shadow appeared, taking on a vaguely humanoid form. It was misshapen, with spikes and barbed wire jutting out from its exposed flesh. It held a pair of curved swords with jagged metal blades and its eyes glowed red. One of the weapons came plunging down before the image faded away.

"I've never seen a demon like that," Daisuke said. "But it certainly fits Golmol's aesthetic. Was it familiar to you?"

"No, Master," Ruq said. "But my interactions with the cult of Golmol are basically zero."

"Hmm, I wonder…" Daisuke trailed off, mind racing. The demon seemed pretty strong, which meant summoning and maintaining it in this reality would be no easy thing. But he knew another source of demons, already summoned, bound, and ready to go. There was no guarantee this was one of the seventy-two, but he was going to have to confirm it before they moved on Sava.

He left the room and caught up with Helena and Jinx near the nurses' station. He didn't look at the bodies littering the floor. "A demon did this. One of Golmol's, I'm pretty sure."

"How did a demon get here?" Jinx asked.

"Good question," Daisuke said. "My guess? Someone guided it in. Does this place have security cameras?"

"I didn't notice," Helena said. "Why, what are you thinking?"

"I'm thinking someone came up here and released the demon. If that's right, you can compare the faces of the people here with the ones on the recordings. Whoever's missing is our guy."

"*We* can?" Helena said. "What about you?"

"I need to go back to Zurich and check the Book of Wisdom. I want to confirm the demon's identity."

"You think it's one of the seventy-two?" Helena asked.

"I think it's a distinct possibility. I'll meet you back at your hotel when I have the details."

CHAPTER TWENTY-ONE

Helena watched Daisuke vanish into a convenient shadow. He'd be back in Zurich in a few seconds. She hoped he was wrong about the demon being one of the seventy-two. Even on the weaker end, those tended to be powerful.

Whatever it was, they'd have to deal with it. For now they needed to figure out how it got here. She headed back toward the elevators where Rostolov was waiting. Despite her best efforts to ignore the horror show she found herself walking through, Helena couldn't stop thinking about what it must've been like for these poor people.

Sergeant Rostolov waited right where they'd left him, hands clasped behind his back. "Where did your friend go?"

"Back to base to do some research on whatever did this," Helena said. "While he's doing that, I'd like to review any security footage from this floor, both before and during the attack."

"Not a problem," Rostolov said. "We've got a tech in the security room as we speak. I'll take you there."

They got into the elevator and rode down to the ground floor. A few twists and turns through back halls normally inaccessible to the public brought them to a room filled with computers, DVRs, and all manner of technical things that she felt certain Crystal would recognize, but that she didn't understand in the least.

A lone technician looked up from his keyboard as they entered. "Sergeant?" He spoke in English which Helena appreciated.

"Is the footage ready for review?" Rostolov asked.

"Yes, sir. I've got it cued up to a few hours before the incident."

"Let's see it."

The tech hit play. It ran at three times normal speed and for several long minutes nothing seemed amiss. Doctors, nurses and patients went about their routines. Then the elevator door opened and a man in a white lab coat stepped out. He glanced around then vanished only to be replaced by a dark, tortured humanoid demon wielding jagged, two-foot-long swords.

The demon began its slaughter, moving from room to room with an unchanging expression on its corpselike face. The only change to its appearance was the amount of blood dripping off its weapons.

Rostolov muttered what sounded like a prayer in Ukrainian before asking, "What in heaven's name is that thing?"

"A demon. Daisuke is hoping to figure out which one."

After what felt like an eternity, the demon returned to its starting point. In a flicker, the demon vanished and the man in the lab coat reappeared in its place. The man straightened his tie, seeming wholly untroubled about the carnage around him, and got into the elevator.

When the doors had slid shut behind him Helena said, "That's enough. We need to find out who that is."

The tech nodded, fingers flying across the keys. "I can isolate his face and run it through our databases. If he has a record, we'll find him."

"Excellent. I'd like a copy of that image as well." Helena figured Crystal might have access to some places the police didn't. Given the circumstances, she didn't want to leave any stone unturned.

The tech glanced at Rostolov, who nodded. "Whatever they need, they get, understood?"

"Yes, sir. It'll take a couple minutes to isolate and enhance the image. I can email it to you when it's ready."

"That's fine." Rostolov led them out into the hall. The air felt wonderfully cool after the heat of the computer room. "Can you beat that thing?"

"We don't have enough details to answer that yet, but I'm confident we'll find a way." That way likely being Daisuke, the same as it always seemed to be. "For now, let's focus on finding the accomplice. He might have valuable information about Sava."

D aisuke stepped out of a shadow into the arrival room at the Circle's base. It was the only place in the building where you could arrive magically and then only if you knew how the magic worked. Daisuke was one of a handful of people who did. The space was only the size of a large closet and he was happy to move out into the hall.

He didn't even have time to take a step before the boss's head popped out of her office door. "What are you doing back already?"

"I need to look at the Book of Wisdom. A demon wiped out all the people Helena rescued, along with the staff of an entire floor of the hospital. It looked like one of Golmol's and I want to confirm if it's one of the seventy-two."

She waved him in and moved to the chair behind her desk. The Book of Wisdom, as always, sat on the corner. She opened the heavy, leather-bound tome, flipped through the pages, then spun it around to face him.

"This is Golmol's section. Take your time and be sure."

Daisuke paged through the demonic illustrations, each more gruesome than the last, until he froze. On the final page of the section was an exact sketch of the demon.

"This is it," Daisuke said. "Karnal the Slaughterer. Kind of a stupid name, but it's a solid tier five demon which is nothing to sneeze at."

The boss's phone chimed and she glanced at the screen. "It's Helena. They got a potential lead on the one responsible for letting the demon in."

"That was quick."

She nodded and scrolled further. "Helena is less than confident in the police force's facial recognition system. She sent a picture and a request to have Crystal take a look as well."

"Good idea," Daisuke said.

The boss stood and headed for the door. "I'll brief Crystal."

Then she was gone, leaving Daisuke alone with the Book of Wisdom. He read the entire entry, but it didn't tell him much. Karnal was essentially a physical force. It liked chopping its victims up and leaving them torn apart. He knew that from visiting the crime scene. It had the usual demonic resistances and that was about it.

Not that it wasn't enough. A demon of that power along with a hellpriest had him outclassed. Daisuke's ego wasn't so big that he'd refuse to admit his limits.

No, if he was going to win this, he needed an edge. Something to even the playing field.

And he knew where to find it: the vault.

"You think she's going to let you take the orb out of safe-keeping?" Ruq asked.

"The boss is reasonably reasonable about this sort of thing. Sneaking past the clan so I can charge it at the fire shrine will be the real trick. Heaven knows they aren't going to let me have access out of the goodness of their hearts, despite all I've done for them."

"Your family is certainly stubborn," Ruq said.

Stubborn or not, given what was at stake, he couldn't take no for an answer.

CHAPTER TWENTY-TWO

D aisuke left the Circle's mountain vault, elemental orb in hand. It was a relief when he moved beyond the magic dead zone. Being unable to see or touch the ether was such a strange feeling. The magic had been a part of him for as long as he could remember and being without it felt weird.

The clear crystal of the orb twinkled in the afternoon sun. As he'd expected, the boss hadn't hesitated to give him permission to use it. She was remarkably practical for a former angel. It was one of the things Daisuke liked best about her.

He sighed and slipped the orb into his satchel. In hindsight, draining it completely before putting it into storage hadn't been the best idea, but that was life. Charging it again shouldn't be a problem, assuming his family didn't feel the need to try and stop him.

Ruq settled on his shoulder as he walked toward a nearby clump of trees. The imp absolutely refused to enter the magic dead zone a second time and Daisuke didn't blame him. Ruq lost all his magical protections and abilities in the zone.

"Are you sure this is a good idea?" Ruq asked. "You and the spirits aren't on the best terms."

"Good terms or not, the bastards owe me, and I mean to collect."

He reached the shadow of a huge spruce and stepped into the shadow paths. The journey from Europe to Japan took seconds. Finding the gap in Japan's wards was simple the second time and he soon emerged in the little grove where he met Natsumi what seemed like a long time ago but was only two days.

Now that he was inside the wards, it was a simple matter to make the short trip to the elemental shrine on Mount Fuji. He emerged from the shadow cast by the fire temple and immediately turned invisible. The crystals that illuminated the cavern during the day had dimmed to almost nothing. To compensate, the Kugo security patrols had conjured lights in the form of magical torches. The torches also marked their locations for any watching enemy. None of them were even trying to be stealthy. That much light in the dim cavern was like flashing a neon sign that said "come kill me."

Lucky for them, Daisuke wasn't interested in a confrontation. He worked his way around to the entrance of the temple and found it unguarded. Sloppy, but it worked out for him. The interior hadn't changed. Power crackled around the altar almost like an electric charge.

As he was considering the best way to charge the orb, the world fell away and Daisuke found himself standing in a dark void. Before him hovered a pillar of white flame, a manifestation of the lord of the fire spirits.

"Have you come to steal my power, boy?" the fire king asked.

Daisuke glared at the ruler of all fire spirits. "No. You're going to give it to me."

He felt the spirit's confusion. "And why would I do such a thing?"

Anger blazed through Daisuke and he ripped the gloves from his hands before thrusting his scarred flesh toward the spirit. "Because you owe me! I was kid, innocent and full of faith in you and your kind, and you let me burn!"

The fire king flinched back from his rage. At least that was how Daisuke interpreted the shudder that ran through the pillar of flame.

"I did nothing wrong aside from having the bad luck to be born with the wrong blood."

"I explained—"

"I don't give a damn about your explanations! It's time to repay some of what you owe me. Take heart, I'm going to use your power to burn away a bunch of demons. That's the Kugo clan's founding principle, right? To purge evil with cleansing flame?"

The spirit was silent for a long moment and Daisuke was starting to think he was going to refuse him.

"Very well, boy. Your words are true and your anger righteous. Take my power and use it well."

Daisuke blinked and found himself back in the temple. The elemental orb grew warm as a white glow filled it until it looked like he held a miniature sun. Perfect. With this they'd have a chance against Sava and his pet demons.

"I hope this burns your bitterness away along with the demons you'll face." The fire king's presence faded to nothing.

Daisuke listened hard as he tucked the orb away. After all that he expected to have Kugo wizards rushing his way, but he sensed no reaction from outside. The fire king's power must've blocked them from noticing the confrontation. Convenient for Daisuke.

"You have an appetite for risk, son." Miles appeared from a corner of the temple. Daisuke hadn't sensed him approach. An impressive feat all on its own. It would be entirely too easy to underestimate Miles.

"Did you need something?" Daisuke asked.

"No. I sensed your presence and thought I'd say hello."

"Okay. Hello and good evening. If there's nothing else, I need to leave. A whole mess of demons out in the Russian wastelands needs destroying."

Daisuke headed for the nearest shadow, but Miles blocked his path. "Wait, please. Is it so difficult to imagine that I want a real relationship with my son? All my other children have turned their backs on me. You're my last chance."

Daisuke's grin held no hint of humor, only bitter amusement. "All one hundred and ninety-nine? I'm impressed you managed to find them all and make contact."

Miles was silent as he stared at his feet. He reminded Daisuke of a little kid who'd been caught doing something naughty. Had Daisuke been in a better mood, he would've laughed.

"Wait, let me guess," Daisuke said. "You only contacted the ones with sufficient magic potential to make them worthwhile in a fight. The rest of my half brothers and sisters didn't even warrant a call."

Miles winced. "There are so many. I needed a limiting principle. I figured the wizards would be the only ones with whom I'd have anything in common and so would have the best chance of sharing a real relationship."

Daisuke shook his head. Miles would never win a father of the year award. "I don't have time to indulge whatever you think our relationship should be. When the world is safe, maybe we can figure something out, but right now I need to go. Take care."

"When the world is safe?" Miles offered a humorless laugh. "That's another way of saying never."

Daisuke shrugged. "Take it however you like."

With that, he stepped into a nearby shadow and vanished into the shadow paths. There were demons waiting and it was time to get back to work.

CHAPTER TWENTY-THREE

Daisuke stepped out of the shadow paths and into Helena's shabby hotel room. Both women were seated on their beds and fiddling with their phones. They looked up a moment after he arrived.

"What took you so long?" Helena asked.

"I made a quick trip to Japan. The boss let me borrow the elemental orb and I charged it with fire magic direct from the fire king. It should help balance the odds a bit. I also confirmed that the demon is one of the seventy-two. He's the weakest of Golmol's nine, but still a solid tier five. Even with the orb, this is not going to be an easy fight."

"I didn't think it would be," Helena said. "I'm also surprised your family let you talk to the fire king."

Daisuke grinned. "I didn't ask for permission. What did you learn about Sava's accomplice?"

"We learned he's not in the police records," Helena said. "Crystal had better luck. She found a businessman named Ivankov who matched his description. He's got to be the man Petruk mentioned when we questioned him."

"No doubt. We'll need to deal with him first, then go after Sava in Staryol."

Helena frowned. "What if Sava uses the transference spell to swap Ivankov with the demon?"

"We should be so lucky," Daisuke said. "Facing Karnal alone—"

Jinx giggled then slapped a hand over her mouth when they both looked at her. "Sorry, but is the demon's name really Karnal?"

Daisuke nodded. "Karnal the Slaughterer, and don't feel bad, that was pretty much my reaction when I saw his name. Anyway, as I was saying, if Sava swaps Karnal for Ivankov it will let us face the demon on his own instead of having to fight him along with a hellpriest and a small army of thralls."

"I hadn't thought of that," Helena said.

"The real danger," Daisuke said. "Is Sava pulling a body swap with Ivankov and slipping away. If that happens, we'd end up having to hunt him down all over again. Not a prospect that thrills me."

Helena stood. "Solid points. We'll go after Ivankov first then. The main problem is that Ivankov's a private citizen. Technically, the police need to arrest him for a trial."

Daisuke's lips twisted. "You think the cops will care what happens to Ivankov after what he helped do at the hospital? Do you care?"

Helena hesitated to answer. She couldn't seriously be thinking the guy deserved anything but a quick end. "We're supposed to be the good guys."

Daisuke ran a hand through his hair and prayed for patience. "We are the good guys. Good guys kill the bad guys. This asshole participated in the murder of scores of innocents and runs a human trafficking operation that has spread untold suffering. Killing this prick is cosmic house cleaning."

"I know, I know." Helena blew out a breath. "Let's just get it over with."

They took the elevator to the first floor, went outside, and flagged down a taxi. The driver spoke enough English to understand where they wanted to go and took off. Daisuke ended up sandwiched between the ladies which made for a nice ride.

The cab slowed as they approached a high-rise apartment building built in a fancy style with decorative gargoyles and polished steel accents. It was the first nice building he'd seen since arriving in Odessa. Clearly the place was meant for a wealthy crowd.

They got out and Helena paid the driver. "Ivankov's on the top floor."

Daisuke whistled. "Human trafficking must pay well."

They strode through a gold-trimmed revolving door and headed for the elevators at the rear of the lobby. A burly guard in a too-tight security uniform stood in front of them, clipboard in hand. He gave Daisuke bouncer vibes.

The guard asked something in Ukrainian.

Daisuke shook his head. "Sorry, no speak the language."

"I asked if you're expected," the guard said with a very faint accent.

"I hope not." Daisuke hit him with a paralysis spell, locking his body in place. "Don't worry, we know where we're going."

Daisuke's gaze bore into the bound guard. "Mr. Ivankov doesn't wish to be disturbed. Make sure no one bothers him until he tells you otherwise."

The powerful psychic command settled in and Daisuke nodded to himself.

Jinx pressed the elevator call button. "Do you think more security's waiting upstairs?"

"I expect so." Daisuke yawned. "If there's one thing guys like Ivankov enjoy, it's having big guys with guns standing between them and anyone who wants to hurt them. Would you like to throw some shadow webs on anyone standing outside his door?"

Jinx beamed. "Sure! I don't feel like I've been much help on this mission."

"I doubt that's true," Daisuke said.

Helena watched their casual conversation with her mouth partway open as if in disbelief of what she was hearing. She really did take things too seriously sometimes. If you were this tense during the easy parts of the mission, what would you do when it hit the fan?

The elevator dinged open. Four guards, armed with machine guns as he expected, stood outside an apartment door. They didn't even have time to react before Jinx's black webs wrapped them up from head to toe. They collapsed, unmoving, on the floor.

"Good job." Daisuke stepped over them and snapped his fingers, popping the lock before pushing it open and walking in like he owned the place.

A man he assumed to be Ivankov sat on the living room couch, engrossed in the evening news, his blond hair slicked back and wearing an impeccably tailored suit. He barely had time to register their intrusion before Daisuke hit him with a paralysis that locked his muscles in place.

Angry blue eyes glared at Daisuke as he approached. He sat on the coffee table directly in front of Ivankov and cast a domination spell. When Daisuke released the paralysis spell, Ivankov's expression slackened, his eyes glazing over.

Good, he was fully under.

"What's your connection to Sava Rude?" Daisuke asked.

"Master," Ivankov said, his voice rich and deep despite being nothing but a monotone. "Teaching me the Way of Pain."

So he was a disciple on his way to becoming a priest. Good thing they were dealing with him now.

"Why did you kill the former prisoners?"

"Feared they might know something. The dead tell no tales."

Daisuke smiled at his ignorance. For a skilled necromancer, the dead could tell many tales. "Tell me about Sava's pet demon."

"Karnal, he's bound to serve by the seal."

"You've seen the seal?" Daisuke asked.

"Once, in Master Sava's workshop under Staryol."

Daisuke turned to Helena. "Did you know he had a workshop under the town?"

"He offered to show us his workshop, but I thought it unwise to take a look. I can't say I'm shocked to learn it's underground."

"Do you have any other questions?" Daisuke asked.

"I can't think of anything," Helena said.

He turned to Jinx but she shook her head.

"Okay." Daisuke snapped his fingers and Ivankov collapsed like a puppet with the strings cut. "That pretty much takes care of things here. I just need to tie up the final loose end."

Daisuke held up his right index finger and a black inchworm made of dark energy appeared on it. He touched

Ivankov's motionless body on the chest and the worm vanished into his body.

"What was that spell?" Jinx asked.

"A dark worm. It'll work its way to Ivankov's heart and when I give the command it'll burst, making it look like an aneurysm. The process is painless." Daisuke added that last bit for Helena, who was favoring him with a disapproving glare.

"If you're going to kill him," Helena said. "Why not do it now and have it over with?"

"You can't cast a translocation spell without a strong connection to the target. If I kill Ivankov, Sava is sure to sense it. I'd just as soon keep the element of surprise. As soon as we arrive and engage Sava, I'll trigger the worm, cutting off his escape route."

Helena winced. "I didn't even think about that. My brain is clearly not in the game. Sorry, both of you."

"Don't worry about it," Daisuke said. "We're a team. Covering each other's weaknesses is part of the deal. So, where's your rental truck?"

"The parking garage at the hotel," Helena said.

"Perfect." He scooped her up, drawing a surprised yelp. "Let's go."

He stepped into a shadow with Jinx right behind him.

CHAPTER TWENTY-FOUR

Even after hearing Helena's description of Staryol, Daisuke was impressed with how bleak the place looked. Everything was dead from the trees to the grass to the locals. The peeling paint on the rotted houses looked like dead skin. You could film a horror movie here without changing a thing. It was the perfect home for demon worshippers.

The pickup rumbled to a stop and Daisuke, Helena, and Jinx climbed out. Daisuke took in the dreary sights and turned to Helena. "And you say I never take you anywhere nice."

"Funny." Helena's gaze darted all around, her head on a swivel.

The ambient corruption wasn't as bad as Castle Raven-claw, but it wasn't pleasant either. At a minimum, it wouldn't interfere with his magic and with the battle on the horizon, Daisuke cared about nothing else.

"Does it seem worse now?" Jinx asked. "Or did I just not notice how awful this place was the first time?"

"It's definitely worse," Helena said. "It's like Sava isn't trying to hide what this place is anymore. I'm not sure if that's a good thing or a bad thing."

"Assume it's a bad thing," Daisuke said. "That's usually the safest bet."

Shuffling footsteps heralded the thralls' arrival. The minor demons came shambling into view from every direction and quickly encircled the group.

"Steady," Daisuke said when he sensed Helena getting ready to attack. "We have to confirm the hellpriest is here first. And no matter what happens, make sure neither of you leave my side."

The thralls parted, ending the conversation. A figure emerged, swathed in black robes laced with glinting barbed wire that sliced his flesh with each step. Crimson trickles stained his skin and the fabric of his robe. Corruption crackled around his body. If his fashion choices hadn't confirmed this was a hellpriest of Golmol, that aura would've.

Sava paused a few feet away and cocked his head as he focused on Daisuke. "Are you her employer? I expected someone older. If you want your ships protected, my prices are non-negotiable."

A faint smile curved Daisuke's lips. "I'm not here to negotiate."

He snapped his fingers, activating the black worm he'd left in Ivankov's chest.

Sava flinched and Daisuke took the opportunity to ready the elemental orb. It glowed white, pulsing with power as if eager to burn away the evil surrounding them.

At his mental command, an inferno of white flames roared out, engulfing Sava and his thralls. The thralls were instantly incinerated, crumbling to ash and blown away by the firestorm. When the flames ebbed, only Sava remained standing amidst the smoldering ruins, singed but unharmed.

"Impressive." Sava brushed some of the ash from the sleeve of his scorched robe. "And I sense you killed my disciple. Remarkably thorough given that we've never met. Usually only people who know me want to kill me this badly."

Daisuke grinned back. "I didn't want you trying to escape."

Sava's laugh had a mad tinge to it. "Escape? You think *I* need to escape from *you*?"

Sava reached into the folds of his robe and pulled out a familiar stone seal marked with an intricate sigil. Karnal's control seal.

Daisuke tensed, fingers tightening around the elemental orb. He had to time this perfectly. Beside him, Helena and Jinx both gathered ether, readying to cast at a moment's notice.

Sava thrust the seal at them, his voice rising to a guttural shout. "Karnal! Kill them all!"

Darkness swirled around before solidifying into a humanoid figure dressed in tattered robes and armed with twin jagged-edged swords of Hell-forged black iron. Spikes and hooks pierced the demon's flesh, making it look more like a torture victim than a perpetrator.

The instant Karnal fully coalesced, Daisuke triggered the orb again. White flames formed a hollow pillar with Karnal in the center, trapping him in place. An effort of will added divine energy to the fire prison, making it even harder for the demon to escape.

Karnal snarled, lashing out with his swords. They glanced

off the barrier, seeming to do no damage but actually scraping away a bit of pure ether with each strike. The demon kept up a steady barrage of silent blows.

"You can't hold him forever!" Sava's face twisted in fury as he turned to flee, black robes swirling. He soon vanished into the labyrinth of abandoned buildings. Daisuke stayed calm. Ruq was keeping an eye on things from the air. He couldn't sneak away on foot.

Unfortunately, Sava wasn't wrong about the barrier. It wasn't going to last forever. Lucky for them it didn't have to.

"Helena." Daisuke pressed the orb into her hands. "Maintain the barrier. Keep the flow of ether steady, the orb will do the rest. Jinx, stay with her in case anything else unpleasant shows up."

Helena didn't look all that confident, but she gripped the orb tight and, aside from a faint wavering of the fire prison, nothing happened.

"What about you?" Jinx asked, her voice rising with fear.

"I need to finish Sava and find Karnal's prison. I'm counting on you to keep Helena safe."

Jinx clenched her fist. "I will, don't worry."

Daisuke grinned and sprinted after Sava.

Ruq, where did he go?

The house to your right, the sort-of-blue one.

I see it. Thanks.

Daisuke veered toward the building. He paused at the door and summoned his trunk before retrieving the Staff of Law. He suspected every bit of extra power he could muster would be needed for this battle.

With a final steadying breath, Daisuke stepped into the building. Rotted floorboards groaned beneath his feet but it didn't seem in danger of collapse. He worked his way forward, staff leading.

Daisuke expected some kind of monster to jump out at him at any moment, but nothing troubled him. At last he reached a staircase to the basement. An eerie glow from below made him nauseous, but also made it easy to see the steps.

At the bottom, a sprawling chamber far bigger than the house above opened up before him. This had to be the workshop Helena mentioned.

Torture devices of all sorts decorated the walls. Razored manacles hung beside a rack, an iron maiden, and more exotic things he didn't want to study too closely. To an item they were encrusted with the blood of past victims. Many past victims if the psychic weight of the room was any indication.

At the far end of the chamber, a black altar sat beneath a grotesque statue of Golmol the Torturer. The details weren't well made, but the hooks and blades hanging from the statue's belt were clear enough. Of greatest interest was the bronze urn resting in the center of the altar. Karnal's prison he felt certain.

Sava himself stood in front of the altar, facing Daisuke. He seemed calmer than he had any right to be. Maybe he had made peace with meeting his master face to face.

Daisuke stalked forward, the Staff of Law at the ready.

"What, no witty banter to offer before we fight?" Sava asked.

"No." Daisuke hurled a bolt of black lightning right at Sava's chest.

The blast was turned aside by some defensive magic, but

the impact sent Sava tumbling over the altar and the prison to the floor.

Giving him no chance to recover, Daisuke hit Sava again and again, driving him back until he was against the statue of Golmol.

The lunatic just laughed as if he was having the time of his life. Given that he was into pain, maybe he was.

Sava threw a hand forward and black chains shot out of nowhere.

Daisuke dove out of the way with inches to spare.

He rolled to his feet and a snap of his fingers sent a blade of white light streaking down at Sava. It hit a barrier a foot from his body and fizzled.

The hellpriest laughed again. "Holy magic has no power in this place."

Well, it had been worth a shot.

Daisuke dodged more black chains as he gathered a larger mass of ether.

He charged Sava, shaping the spell as he did.

A chain slashed his cheek, drawing a wince but not slowing him.

When he reached the hellpriest, he swung the staff with all his might, releasing the power at the same time. The impact rang like a thunderclap.

Sava flew across the chamber and hammered into the iron maiden, getting impaled on a number of spikes in the process. As he staggered to his feet, Daisuke raced after him.

A sharp front kick drove Sava deeper into the iron maiden. Daisuke slammed the door, impaling him in hundreds of places.

From within Sava continued his insane laughter.

"Laugh at this." Daisuke opened a black portal and

flooded the iron maiden with lightning. He didn't stop until he could no longer sense any life within.

A few moments of silence passed before he pulled the iron maiden open. What was left of Sava's body tumbled out. He wasn't pretty before and now he looked like he got run through a giant meat tenderizer. Which wasn't totally wrong if you were being honest.

He kicked the body over and pulled the demon seal out. A burst of flame burned the blood off of it. He touched it to the staff and said, "By the blood of Solomon that flows through my veins, I command you to merge."

A smooth spot formed on the staff and Karnal's rune appeared on it.

Daisuke hurried back to the altar and collected the prison from where it had fallen. Okay, he had everything he needed. Helena had to be getting tired so no time to screw around.

Who was he kidding? It was taking all Daisuke had to put one foot in front of the other.

He shook his weariness off and retraced his steps back outside.

The pillar of flame was still burning bright. Through the flicker of fire he caught an occasional glimpse of a very pissed-off demon. Well, if it was mad now, wait until it was back in its prison.

He made his way to the far side of the pillar and found Helena plastered with sweat and breathing hard. The orb had lost nearly all of its glow. Looked like he hadn't finished his business any too soon. Jinx kept a grim eye on the surrounding village.

"You did great," Daisuke said when he reached them. "Give me the orb."

"Gladly." Helena passed it over and immediately hit her knees.

Jinx hurried over and put an arm around her. "Are you okay?"

Daisuke ignored them and focused. First he willed the fire to vanish. As soon as it did he said, "Karnal, by my blood and the power of the staff you are bound. Halt!"

The demon froze. Even as it tried to resist, he could tell this creature's power was nothing compared to Vorgon's.

"By my will and the power of the seal be bound. By the blood of Solomon and might of the Staff of Law, Karnal be bound in bronze!" He tapped the prison with the staff and glowing chains shot out, wrapped around Karnal, and dragged it toward the opening.

The demon fought and Daisuke endured its rage and corruption. The process was as familiar as it was wearying and after a minute of exertion, Karnal was fully imprisoned once more.

Now for the final spell. "Darkness bound in bronze, blood compels and the staff commands, be sealed away for all time."

The open top of the prison fused shut and a little indentation the exact size of the seal formed on top. It was done and thank goodness for that.

Daisuke sat in the blackened dirt, too tired to move. Ruq appeared in rat form and landed in his lap. "That went reasonably well."

Daisuke managed a weak laugh. "Easy for you to say. But we won so I won't complain."

"You both need to rest," Jinx said. "Let's get out of this awful place."

Daisuke sighed and shook his head, the motion sending

pain lancing through his skull. "Not yet. We need to check the workshop for dangerous artifacts. We'll rest here for a few hours then I'll go back and have a last look around."

Jinx didn't look thrilled but she finally said, "Okay. I'll keep watch. You just take it easy."

Taking it easy was about all Daisuke was up to at the moment so he didn't argue. He did drag himself over beside Helena who was on her back staring at the sky. They shifted around until her head was lying on his lap.

"Was this a win?" Helena asked. "So many people died I'm not sure."

He sighed and stroked her hair. "I'm not sure winning is a thing in real life. We survived this particular bad guy and he and his friends didn't. Plus we've got another demon for the vault. I'm content with that result."

"I guess I'll have to be as well." She didn't sound like she meant it, but Daisuke couldn't do anything about that. Helena, for all her talent as a field agent and wizard, had always been softer than was prudent for someone in this line of work.

EPILOGUE

Daisuke yawned and strode down the street toward Arcane Books and Trinkets. He couldn't begin to describe how glad he was to be back in Zurich. A search of Sava's workshop temple yielded little in the way of valuable magic. The handful of cursed items were now locked up safe in the vault along with Karnal's prison and the elemental orb which was once again drained of power. He'd be happy if they didn't need to use it again as he had no desire to speak with the spirits again.

Helena and Jinx had remained behind in Odessa to help the police with a final wrap-up. He didn't think it was strictly necessary, but Helena insisted on explaining everything to Rostolov. As always with Helena, some things were worth arguing about and other things weren't. This fell into the latter category. The ladies should be back tomorrow and then he suspected they would all be on their way to Istanbul to hunt down the final demon Remi sold.

Hopefully that went more smoothly than the last mission.

"I bet you a dozen cookies it'll be a complete shitshow,"

Ruq said. The imp was riding, invisible, on his shoulder. At least he remembered to keep his voice low enough that none of the other pedestrians gave them a second look.

"No bet. Besides, you don't have any money nor can you bake. How did you plan to pay up if I won?"

"We've been on enough of these jobs that I'm confident it wouldn't be an issue."

Daisuke rolled his eyes but couldn't argue. That said, he dearly hoped things went quickly. He was much more interested in whatever had Ahmed so obsessed with the Sinai. Those were the sort of magical mysteries that got his blood pumping.

They rounded a corner and headed for the back door of the Circle's headquarters. He let himself in and turned toward the boss's office. A quick knock was answered with a prompt, "Come in."

He pushed the door open and took his usual seat in front of the boss's desk. She was studying what looked like satellite images of the desert. He saw nothing of even remote interest in any of them.

"Is it done?" she asked.

"Yup, Karnal is locked away along with all of Sava's toys. I swear these pricks collect more useless crap. It's hardly worth taking most of it."

"However useless it might be to you, it's still better to keep it out of the hands of some other wannabe hellpriest."

Daisuke shrugged. "If you say so. What are those?"

She spun the images around so he could take a better look. They weren't any more interesting right side up. "These are satellite images from an area of the Sinai Peninsula where there was supposed to be an old Crusader fortress. As you can see, something is missing."

"No kidding." He spun the pictures back around. "Why are we interested in Crusader ruins again?"

"We're not interested in them specifically. I told Crystal to search the area for anything of note. Unless you're into terrorist camps, this was the most worthwhile thing she found. We know the ruins are supposed to be present. Some archaeologists were exploring the area two years ago trying to find them and ended up taken hostage."

"What kind of idiot archeologist visits a wasteland filled with terrorists?" he asked.

"Focus, Daisuke. The important thing is that some magic is concealing the ruins from our satellite. Why would someone do that if there wasn't something interesting going on?"

"Beats me. You think this is what had Ahmed so excited?"

"No way to say for sure, but it seems like a good place to start looking."

"Okay, do you want me to check it out before or after I deal with the demon in Istanbul?"

The boss touched her chin as she thought. "Istanbul first. Anatoly is back in Egypt trying to dig up more background on Ahmed and the orb. When you're finished with the demon, join him there. Helena and Jinx will join you two once they've recovered from the last mission."

Daisuke could've used a little more time to recover himself, but he didn't bother pointing that out. While welcome, the rest wasn't a necessity.

"I'll leave tomorrow. Do you have a local contact I can work with?"

"Stop by the shop in the morning. I'll have the details ready for you then." Almost as an afterthought she said, "Good work on this last job."

Daisuke grinned. "All part of the service, Boss. See you tomorrow."

He left her office and yawned. Less than a day to rest and stuff himself with carbs. Well, it could've been worse. She might've ordered him to leave today.

He cracked his knuckles. Maybe they'd find some good stuff in those ruins. Nothing like the prospect of magical treasure to get a wizard excited.

AUTHOR NOTE

Hello everyone,

It was another rough one for Daisuke and the gang and things aren't going to get any better with things continue in The Cursed Fortress.

If you don't want to miss any of my new releases, deals, general news about the Etherverse, you can signup for my newsletter on my website.
    www.jamesewisher.com

Until next time, thanks for reading,

James E. Wisher

ALSO BY JAMES E. WISHER

The 72 Demons

The Blood of Solomon

A Friend in Need

The Demon Masks

Hunt For The Devil Man

A Family Reunion

The Cursed Fortress (Coming in 2026)

The Aegis of Merlin:

The Impossible Wizard

The Awakening

The Chimera Jar

The Raven's Shadow

Escape From the Dragon Czar

Wrath of the Dragon Czar

The Four Nations Tournament

Death Incarnate

Atlantis Rising

Rise of the Demon Lords

The Pale Princess

Malice

Hearts of Corrupt Fire

Ultima Thule

Aegis of Merlin Omnibus Vol 1.

Aegis of Merlin Omnibus Vol 2.

The Complete Aegis of Merlin Omnibus

Summoned to Another Words and Forced to Fight The Demon King

The Summoned Hero

The Birth of Ronin

The Fate of The Five Kingdoms

The Plague Lands

Elfhome

The Immortal Apprentice Trilogy

The War With Audin (Prequel Novella)

The Hunt For Revenge

The Army of Darkness

The Apprentice Reborn

The Soul Bound Saga

An Unwelcome Journey

Darkness in Tiber

Depths of Betrayal

The Black Iron Empire

Overmage

The Divine Key Trilogy

Shadow Magic

For The Greater Good

The Divine Key Awakens

The Portal Wars Saga

The Hidden Tower

The Great Northern War

The Portal Thieves

The Master of Magic

The Chamber of Eternity

The Heart of Alchemy

The Sanguine Scroll

Shadow of The Dragons

The Dragonspire Chronicles

The Black Egg

The Mysterious Coin

The Dragons' Graveyard

The Slave War

The Sunken Tower

The Dragon Empress

The Dragonspire Chronicles Omnibus Vol. 1

The Dragonspire Chronicles Omnibus Vol. 2

The Complete Dragonspire Chronicles Omnibus

Soul Force Saga

Disciples of the Horned One Trilogy:

Darkness Rising

Raging Sea and Trembling Earth

Harvest of Souls

Disciples of the Horned One Omnibus

Chains of the Fallen Arc:

Dreaming in the Dark

On Blackened Wings

Chains of the Fallen Omnibus

The Complete Soul Force Saga Omnibus

Other Fantasy Novels:

The Squire

Death and Honor Omnibus

The Rogue Star Series:

Children of Darkness

Children of the Void

Children of Junk

Rogue Star Omnibus Vol. 1

Children of the Black Ship

Children of The End

ABOUT THE AUTHOR

James E. Wisher is a writer of science fiction and Fantasy novels. He's been writing since high school and reading everything he could get his hands on for as long as he can remember.